INSIDE THE WORLDS OF
STAR WARS®
EPISODE I

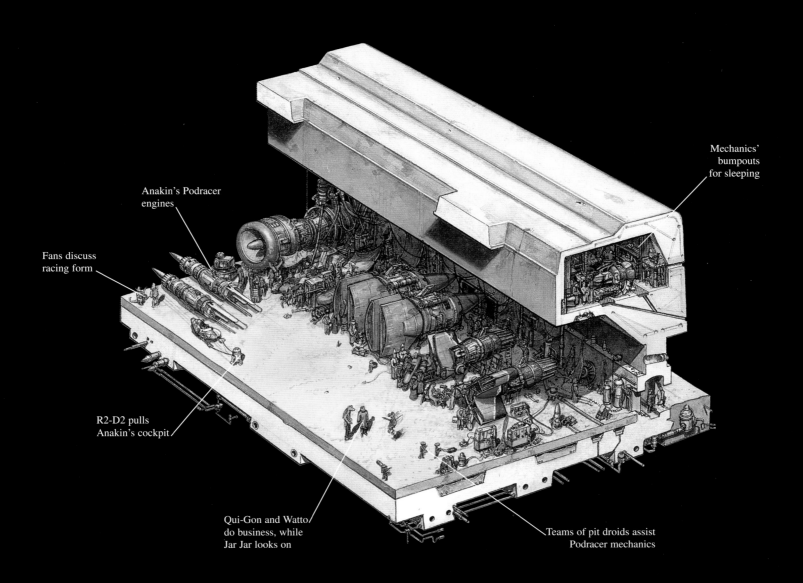

Mechanics' bumpouts for sleeping

Anakin's Podracer engines

Fans discuss racing form

R2-D2 pulls Anakin's cockpit

Qui-Gon and Watto do business, while Jar Jar looks on

Teams of pit droids assist Podracer mechanics

INSIDE THE WORLDS OF

STAR WARS

EPISODE I ®

WRITTEN BY

KRISTIN LUND

ILLUSTRATED BY

HANS JENSSEN

&

RICHARD CHASEMORE

www.starwars.com   www.dk.com

CONTENTS

THE GALAXY

HE TIME OF EPISODE I, the Galactic Republic has enjoyed centuries of peace under
guardianship of the Jedi Knights. Countless species make up a magnificent
onwealth of civilizations that thrive throughout the galaxy's millions of worlds.
st are integrated into the Republic through trade and the sharing of each other's
res, and participate in the Republic's great ideals by being represented in the
ic Senate. However, peace and prosperity have made the Republic complacent;
s are appearing in its foundations as corruption takes its toll on civic life. The
of Episode I are intrinsically caught up with the drama unfolding at the heart of
ublic. Naboo, Tatooine, and Coruscant could not be less alike. But despite their
ces, their fates intertwine with that of Anakin Skywalker, the young boy whose
life holds the galaxy's destiny in the balance.

SCALE: 1 DIVISION = 5,000 LIGHT YEARS

PPROXIMATELY 100,000 light years in diameter. It includes over one million inhabited worlds and thousands of diverse, intelligent species.
s enormous region of inhabited space was formed nearly five billion years ago by the gravitational collapse of a large cloud of dust and gas.

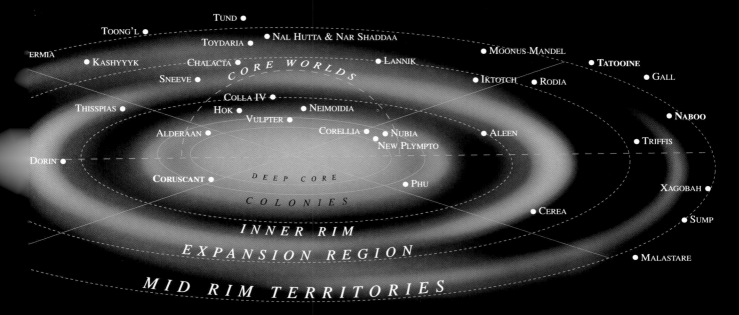

TUND
TOONG'L
TOYDARIA
NAL HUTTA & NAR SHADDAA
ERMIA
KASHYYYK
CHALACTA
CORE WORLDS
LANNIK
MOONUS-MANDEL
TATOOINE
SNEEVE
IKTOTCH
RODIA
GALL
COLLA IV
THISSPIAS
HOK
NEIMOIDIA
VULPTER
NABOO
ALDERAAN
CORELLIA
NUBIA
ALEEN
NEW PLYMPTO
TRIFFIS
DORIN
DEEP CORE
CORUSCANT
PHU
XAGOBAH
COLONIES
CEREA
SUMP
INNER RIM
EXPANSION REGION
MALASTARE
MID RIM TERRITORIES

NABOO has long been an
enigma to astrophysicists. Its
porous, plasma-rich interior
and lack of a molten core is a
phenomenon not found on any
known planet in the galaxy. It is
generally thought, however, that
the plasma (a naturally occurring
form of intense energy unique to
Naboo) is the key to many of the
planet's secrets.

TATOOINE

Distance from Core:	43,000 *light years*
Number of Suns:	2
Number of Moons:	2
Population:	200,000
Surface Water:	1%
Composition:	*Molten core with rocky mantle and silicate rock crust*

TATOOINE is one of three
planets in a binary star
system. As one of the oldest
planets in known space, it has
been studied by scientists
eager to learn the origins of
the galaxy. Fossils bear
testament to its ocean-covered
surface millions of years ago
but today the planet is
covered in arid desert and
prone to vast sand storms.

CORUSCANT orbits relatively
far from its tiny sun, varying
from 207 million to 251 million
km (128 million to 155 million
miles), and thus does not have a
climate particularly suited to
humans. This problem is
overcome by an array of orbital
mirrors that augment the sun's
warmth and light. The first
foundations of the planet-
encompassing Galactic City
were built on a historic
battlefield where three ancient
civilizations fought for control
over the planet. Once largely
covered by oceans, millions of
years of overpopulation on
Coruscant have drained all
natural bodies of water. Polar
cap stations melt ice and
distribute water throughout
Galactic City via a sophisticated
network of pipelines.

CORUSCANT

Distance from Core:	10,000 *light years*
Number of Suns:	1
Number of Moons:	4
Population:	1 trillion
Surface Water:	29% *(in ice caps)*
Composition:	*Molten core with rocky mantle and silicate rock crust*

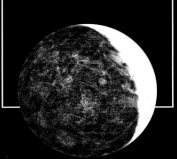

NABOO

NABOO IS A BIZARRE, GEOGRAPHICALLY UNIQUE WORLD located along a major galactic trade route near the Outer Rim. The planet's serene surface of sweeping hills and rolling seas is deceptive: beneath it lies a shadowy underwater world of winding caverns and tunnels inhabited by gigantic, ferocious sea creatures. This immense labyrinth runs through the entire planet, becoming increasingly rocky and dense in the lower strata. The planet's center seethes and bubbles with eruptions of exotic plasmic energy. Over millennia these eruptions form new caverns and tunnels, and influence surface features such as mountains. The planet's two primary civilizations, the Naboo and the Gungans, rely on this plasma power, although they collect and use it in different ways.

The Naboo royal residence, Theed Palace, perches on top of a tremendous cliff with panoramic views of the surrounding countryside.

SECRETS OF OTOH GUNGA

When the amphibious Gungans were forced to retreat underwater in a fierce struggle for territory thousands of years ago, they stumbled upon a secret that enabled them to live there permanently. In deep waters, they came across a strange lifeform known as locap that burrows into porous rock and siphons out plasma. The Gungans found that they were able to extract plasma from the plant using special harvesting bongos (Gungan submarines) equipped with a front-mounted siphon. This natural source of energy has many uses in Gungan life, including the creation of their unique bubble cities. Plasma-based technology allows powerful hydrostatic fields to be generated around basic frameworks, keeping water out but allowing individuals to pass through.

CULTURED CITY

Chancellor Palpatine's shuttle hovers over the elegantly domed buildings of Theed, his home city and the capital of Naboo. From this vantage point Palpatine can admire the city's unified, harmonious style, the result of extensive rebuilding after the upheavals of the ancient past. Theed's sophisticated culture has produced many able and admired galactic politicians, not least of whom is Palpatine himself, who learned much about the mechanics of government and the subtleties of power during his early years here. Naboo's reputation for peace and tolerance in the moral wilderness of the galaxy's Outer Rim lent Palpatine credibility as a young politician. The Naboo now feel secure in a galaxy ruled by this willful individual, however remote and inscrutable he has become.

NABOO LOCATIONS

THE DIVERSE TERRAIN OF NABOO teems with luscious plant and animal life. Whether it's the rich, green plains and insect-ridden swamps of the surface, or the dark, fish-rich depths of the oceans, Naboo offers fruitful existences to those inhabitants who live in harmony with the planet. Several Gungan and Naboo chroniclers have advanced the theory that the mysterious and now long-dead civilization whose ruins dot the countryside failed to respect this balance and were destroyed by their greed.

Lake Paonga, hidden deep in the Naboo swamps, is a secret entrance to the underwater caverns where the Gungan capital city of Otoh Gunga is found.

Great Grass Plains

Cliff edge

Site of Grass Plains Battle

Theed

Underwaterway leads into Solleu River, which runs through Theed

Caves of Eleuabad, one of the most notorious locations of sando aqua monsters

Water-filled underwaterways

Gungan sentry posts

Gallo Mountains

Gungan sacred place

Trade Federation landing site

Jar Jar Binks' adopted homelands

Lianorm Swamp stretches over an area of 85 square kilometers (34 square miles)

Lake Paonga

Otoh Gunga

Entrance to underwaterways from Lake Paonga

Continental slope

NABOO UNDERWATERWAYS

Underneath the surface of Naboo, a tremendous maze of passages and caves, created by movements of unstable plasmic energy in the interior, provides the Gungans with transport routes through the planet. Navigating these underwaterways requires immense skill since they are home to ferocious creatures. A single wrong turn can spell certain death. In spite of the risks, fleets of Gungan trading subs constantly voyage through these routes; overland travel on fambaas or kaadu is slower and more arduous for this amphibious species.

SACRED PLACE

Hidden in the swampy foothills of the Gallo Mountains, the sacred place is a haven of worship for the Gungans and a sanctuary in times of trouble. Scattered around are giant statues and a vast, crumbling temple, relics of a long-extinct race of Naboo inhabitants. The Gungans acknowledge this race as their planet's elders. Yet archeologists are mystified as to the relevance of these crumbling remnants: are they giant representations of the race themselves or are they massive icons devoted to their gods?

Dense foliage cuts off site from outside world

Temple ruins

Tangled roots of cambylictus trees

SOLLEU RIVER

Although the cultures of the Naboo and the Gungans are different in many ways, both share a close relationship with water. The Naboo capital, Theed, is virtually a floating city, nestling on the banks of the mighty Solleu, a river fed by underground tributaries flowing through the planet interior. However, unlike the amphibious Gungans, the Naboo believe the meditative and restorative qualities of flowing water are best appreciated from dry land.

FUNERAL TEMPLE

The Theed Funeral Temple is located in a tranquil spot on the edge of the city. Its open-air design and numerous windows frame a magnificently carved stone platform. Nearby stands the Livet Tower containing an eternal flame, whose never-ending light reminds the Naboo of their own mortality and their duty to lead harmonious lives. Naboo funeral custom dictates that the body of the deceased be cremated within two days of death. In this way, it is believed, the life force of the dead is returned to the planet. Once the ashes are collected, they are carried onto the bridge between the temple and Livet Tower and cast into the Solleu River before it plunges over the cliff.

TURRET ROOM

As active members of the Galactic Republic, the Naboo regularly entertain dignitaries from other worlds in lavish, hand-crafted suites of rooms within Theed Palace. When the Jedi High Council arrive for the funeral of Qui-Gon Jinn they make use of a turret room in which to mourn privately and celebrate the life of their fellow Jedi. This serene chamber is attached to a small temple where Naboo monarchs pay homage to the great rulers of the past. The temple and chamber were built by the first ruler of the Great Time of Peace, King Jafan, who helped reestablish peace on Naboo. It is here that Yoda warns Obi-Wan of the grave dangers he forsees in training Anakin as a Jedi.

GUNGAN SENTRY POST

The huge statue heads that dot the edges of the Lianorm Swamp at the foothills of the Gallo Mountains provide lookouts for Gungan sentries. These soldiers scan the Great Grass Plains using *farseein* (Gungan electrobinoculars). Before the Battle of Naboo, a sentry spies the Naboo Head of Security, Captain Panaka, and a group of volunteers crossing the Great Grass Plains from Theed.

Grazing kaadu

Gungan sentry

Anakin

OTOH GUNGA

ANCHORED TO AN UNDERWATER CLIFF DEEP IN LAKE PAONGA, Otoh Gunga is home to nearly one million inhabitants. Like all Gungan underwater cities, Otoh Gunga's central district is a dense cluster of bubbles made up of elegant city squares, noisy cantinas, oval-shaped sacred bubbles, and an Ancient Quarter, with fragile bubbles that now glow only faintly. Radiating outwards are the Otoh Villages, where most Gungans live and work. At the furthest edges are satellite clusters, some of which have been cast out from other cities and are trying to attach themselves to Otoh Gunga.

Hydrostatic bubbles keep water out but allow individuals to pass through at special portal zones; the bubbles close up behind, like organic membranes

Utanodes project hydrostatic bubble field

Bubbles are partly lit by their own natural glow

Bongos are grown organically by artist-scientists working in an outlying bubble complex. The development of new growth formulas can herald great fame, and bongo organics is a popular course at Gungan braineries (colleges).

Plasma globe maps line the central walkways to aid visitor orientation, although fast-paced new bubble growth means they are mostly out of date

Chemical evaporators in portal zone dry off water from incomers

Bongo sub docking pen receives visitors from all over Otoh Gunga and further afield

REP COUNCIL BOARD ROOM
One of Boss Nass' first acts as Governor was to order the construction of a prestigious new boardroom and suites of offices, many of which have yet to be assigned any purpose.

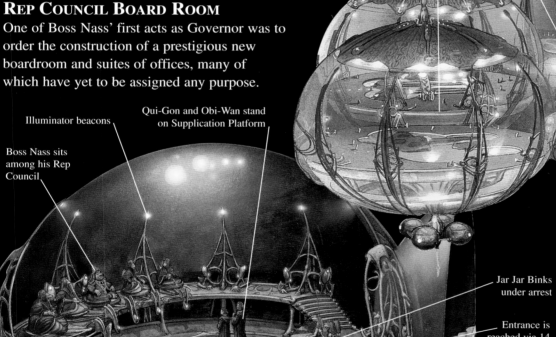

Illuminator beacons

Qui-Gon and Obi-Wan stand on Supplication Platform

Boss Nass sits among his Rep Council

Jar Jar Binks under arrest

Entrance is reached via 14 increasingly grandiose foyer bubbles

Zone of officials' offices, guard stations, and holding cells

Observation walkways

Locap branch

Patrol guard

Bubble wort ampules are activated during the initial growth of the bubble structures

Edge of final foyer bubble

Plasma detonator trained on supplicants

Power control

Field focussing elements

Listening plates give advance warning of sea creatures

Centrifugal pump purifies air using exotic bacteria, which glow as they eat toxins, producing the characteristic Gungan floor glow

Supplementary plasma storage for high-security bubbles

LOCAP FARMING
Locap plants grow very slowly and live for hundreds of years. Their roots bore into porous rock and siphon out plasma, which is naturally stabilized by the plants' digestive processes. This safe form of plasma collects in buds located at the tips of stalks. The Gungans farm plasma from the buds using harvesting subs. This is a dangerous job, as locap buds have circular lobes with spiny teeth that snap shut when any pressure is felt.

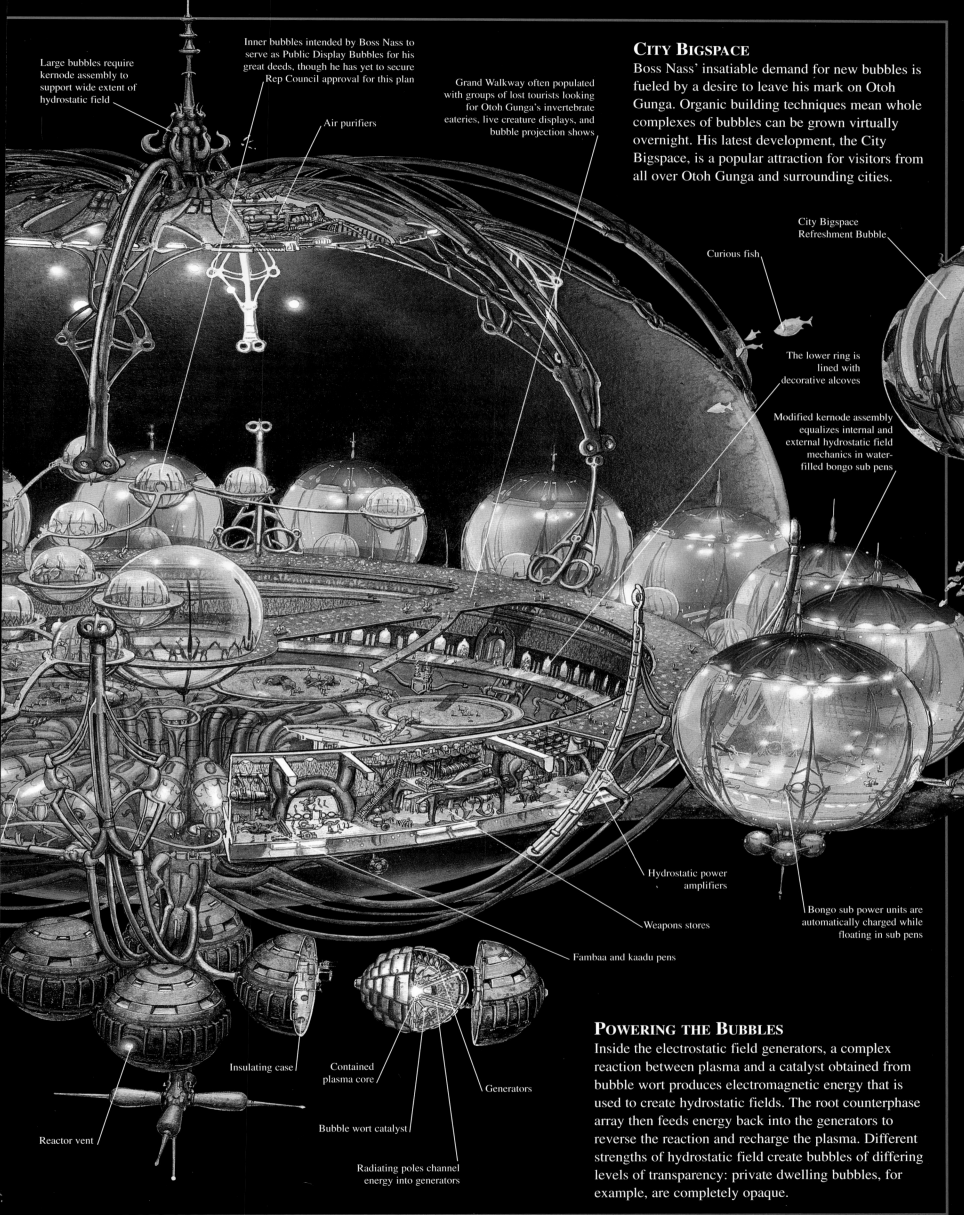

Large bubbles require kernode assembly to support wide extent of hydrostatic field

Inner bubbles intended by Boss Nass to serve as Public Display Bubbles for his great deeds, though he has yet to secure Rep Council approval for this plan

Air purifiers

Grand Walkway often populated with groups of lost tourists looking for Otoh Gunga's invertebrate eateries, live creature displays, and bubble projection shows

CITY BIGSPACE

Boss Nass' insatiable demand for new bubbles is fueled by a desire to leave his mark on Otoh Gunga. Organic building techniques mean whole complexes of bubbles can be grown virtually overnight. His latest development, the City Bigspace, is a popular attraction for visitors from all over Otoh Gunga and surrounding cities.

City Bigspace Refreshment Bubble

Curious fish

The lower ring is lined with decorative alcoves

Modified kernode assembly equalizes internal and external hydrostatic field mechanics in water-filled bongo sub pens

Hydrostatic power amplifiers

Bongo sub power units are automatically charged while floating in sub pens

Weapons stores

Fambaa and kaadu pens

Insulating case

Contained plasma core

Generators

Bubble wort catalyst

Radiating poles channel energy into generators

Reactor vent

POWERING THE BUBBLES

Inside the electrostatic field generators, a complex reaction between plasma and a catalyst obtained from bubble wort produces electromagnetic energy that is used to create hydrostatic fields. The root counterphase array then feeds energy back into the generators to reverse the reaction and recharge the plasma. Different strengths of hydrostatic field create bubbles of differing levels of transparency: private dwelling bubbles, for example, are completely opaque.

DROID CONTROL SHIP

For the trade federation officials who live in it for months on end, the huge Droid Control Ship is an entire world in space. Confinement aboard the converted cargo ship causes frayed nerves and petty backbiting among these merchants of greed. Neimoidians rarely stray far from the command bridge for fear that a colleague will gain some advantage in their absence or form an alliance against them. Equipped with a computer powerful enough to remotely control an entire droid invasion force, this ship is set to launch a determined act of aggression against the virtually defenseless planet of Naboo.

The signal to begin activation of the droid army is given via the pilot's manual controls.

Pilot in navigation station controls ship systems via datagoggles and hand-operated instrument panels

Control signal computer relays commands to droid army

CONTROL SHIP BRIDGE

Dominated by the throne-like pilot navigation station, the control ship bridge is a well-guarded location on a tower at the heart of the spacecraft. Droid pilot operatives are stationed at navigation computers on an underfloor. In this small, confined environment, Trade Federation officials frequently seek the relative privacy of the shadowy corners to scheme against each other, nominally out of earshot (though actually inviting and welcoming attention and suspicion). They communicate with trade partners via a viewscreen situated in a port at one side of the bridge.

SECRET ARMY

Usually piled high with cargo, the cavernous hangars in the control ship have been cleared to allow for the transport and mobilization of a droid invasion army in complete secrecy. The most recent customs officials from the Galactic Republic to venture on board the ship were persuaded that the suspicious-looking components they saw had no military function, but were a shipment of the latest, expensive binary load-lifters. However, the Jedi who emerge from a circulation vent are under no illusions about what they are witnessing.

CONFERENCE ROOM

The control ship's centersphere contains 50 conference rooms. As these rooms are used for trade negotiations, they are specially adapted to place clients at a disadvantage. The adaptations include variable gas emitters and remote-operated "concentration deficit" chairs, which make it difficult for customers to think clearly.

AIR-TRAFFIC CONTROL

The flow of traffic in and out of the ship is monitored from droid stations that overlook the hangars. Despite their slow reaction times, droids now oversee many ship functions. Replacing paid employees and expensive protocol droids with low-maintenance droid "slaves" partially offsets the massive costs of assembling the droid army.

BLAST DOORS

While the Jedi face fearsome droidekas, the Neimoidian Viceroy and his aides cower in the bridge behind triple blast doors. In status-obsessed Neimoidian society, even doors assert social standing, and these bridge doors are particularly elaborate—reminding ship employees of the superiority of its high-level occupants. However, the doors are not as impenetrable as they look, as Qui-Gon proves when he burns through them with his lightsaber.

Jedi emerge from circulation vent

Cargo containers moved aside to make space for droid army

Cargo bay

Row of MTTs (Multi-Troop Transports)

THEED HANGAR

SITTING ATOP THE CLIFF EDGE in the city's central district, the elegant Theed Hangar is a well-guarded military airbase for the N-1 starfighter fleet and Queen Amidala's Royal Starship. The neighboring power generator supplies the spacecraft in the hangar with plasma energy through underground conduits. Equipped with air-traffic control, tactical computer stations, and a secret subterranean tunnel link to the palace, the hangar will play a pivotal role in the Battle of Naboo and become a rallying point for the eventual uprising.

Anticipating no resistance from the peace-loving Naboo—let alone two experienced Jedi—battle droids leave the Royal Starship operational and ready to fly.

Pilot training center

Computer terminals receive coded battle strategies from the palace battle computer and download them into starfighters' computer banks

N-1 starfighter locked into landing position

The Great Hall, where Queen Amidala inspects her troops at ceremonial parades

Guidance beacon

Energy ports deliver high-voltage charges from palace generators

Trade Federation battle tank (AAT)

Central guidance system uses traction mechanics to guide spacecraft into the hangar automatically by locking onto their flight coordinates

Naboo goddess of security and safekeeping

Astromech droid holding area, where utility droids are prepared for onboard flight support assignments

Flight guidance beacon

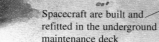

Spacecraft are built and refitted in the underground maintenance deck

Electromag rails generate grav field to reduce speed of incoming spaceships inside hangar

GUIDANCE SYSTEMS

The volunteer pilots of the Royal Naboo Security Forces are trained to use both on-board flight computers and air-traffic control to navigate their fighters into the hangar. However, some veteran pilots are fond of boasting to their juniors that they can gauge the entrance by observing how the wind is affecting the nearby waterfalls.

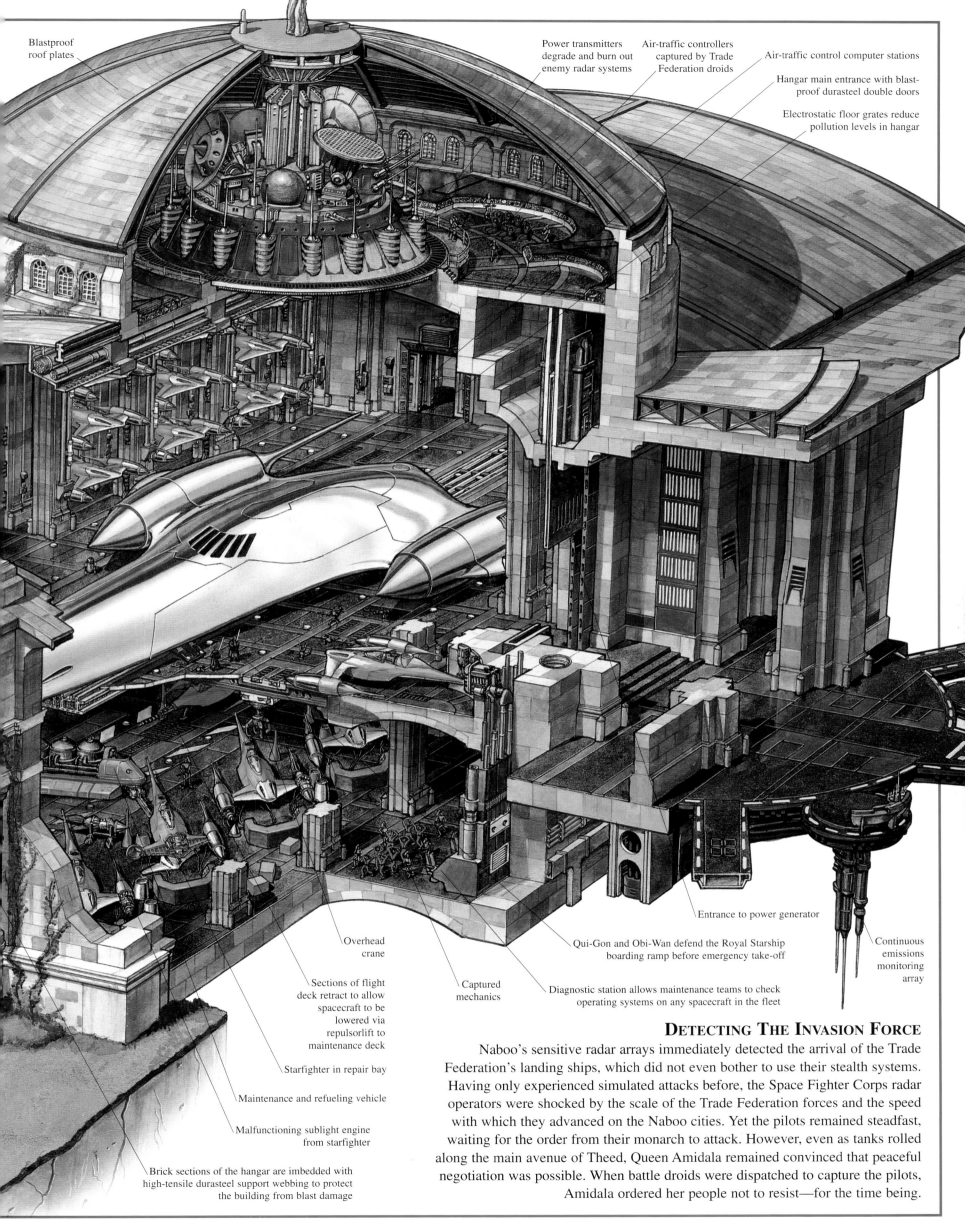

Blastproof
roof plates

Power transmitters
degrade and burn out
enemy radar systems

Air-traffic controllers
captured by Trade
Federation droids

Air-traffic control computer stations

Hangar main entrance with blastproof durasteel double doors

Electrostatic floor grates reduce
pollution levels in hangar

Entrance to power generator

Continuous
emissions
monitoring
array

Qui-Gon and Obi-Wan defend the Royal Starship
boarding ramp before emergency take-off

Overhead
crane

Captured
mechanics

Diagnostic station allows maintenance teams to check
operating systems on any spacecraft in the fleet

Sections of flight
deck retract to allow
spacecraft to be
lowered via
repulsorlift to
maintenance deck

Starfighter in repair bay

Maintenance and refueling vehicle

Malfunctioning sublight engine
from starfighter

Brick sections of the hangar are imbedded with
high-tensile durasteel support webbing to protect
the building from blast damage

DETECTING THE INVASION FORCE

Naboo's sensitive radar arrays immediately detected the arrival of the Trade
Federation's landing ships, which did not even bother to use their stealth systems.
Having only experienced simulated attacks before, the Space Fighter Corps radar
operators were shocked by the scale of the Trade Federation forces and the speed
with which they advanced on the Naboo cities. Yet the pilots remained steadfast,
waiting for the order from their monarch to attack. However, even as tanks rolled
along the main avenue of Theed, Queen Amidala remained convinced that peaceful
negotiation was possible. When battle droids were dispatched to capture the pilots,
Amidala ordered her people not to resist—for the time being.

TATOOINE

I N GALACTIC TERMS, Tatooine is a close neighbor of Naboo. The planets are found on either sides of the boundary between the galaxy's Mid and Outer Rims, yet they could hardly be more different. Naboo is as mild and fertile as Tatooine is stifling and barren, its blazing atmosphere heated by two nearby suns. The planets are far apart in terms of civilization, too. Tatooine's first settlers were poor laborers transported there by mining corporations who believed the planet to be rich in minerals and ores. When the venture failed, the mining companies closed operations and abandoned their workers. Today, a sense of resentment and angry dissatisfaction lingers on in their descendents. With the establishment of hyperspace routes—Tatooine is situated at the nexus of several—the planet also became a refuge for smugglers and outlaws on the run, sealing its reputation for lawlessness and corruption.

TOWN AND COUNTRY

Tatooine's few settlements are separated from each other by vast expanses of desert. The poor standards of living and harsh conditions on Tatooine mean that little distinguishes one town from another. Yet Mos Espa's location near Tatooine's famous Podrace arena gives it a distinctive feel. Along with the usual spacers, its cafés and cantinas buzz with Podrace crews, visiting fans, and professional gamblers. By contrast, rural Tatooine is a lonely world of small moisture farms. These use simple vaporators to collect the tiny amounts of water in the air, which is sold as a commodity and used to irrigate underground plantations.

Tatooine is so fiercely lit by its twin suns that it appears from a certain distance to be a star itself. The planet is uninhabitable save for one relatively cool area of its northern hemisphere.

THE SECRETS OF THE STONES

Characterized by gigantic, top-heavy rocks that rise eerily from the sand, Mushroom Mesa is one of the most astonishing features of Tatooine's desert wasteland. Many observers have noted the humanoid faces that appear in some of the stones: a freak accident of wind erosion or ritual objects carved by alien hands, no one knows. Some observers believe the secret lies with the Sand People, who, they note, avoid the Mesa as if it were cursed. Tatooine's more recent settlers are less superstitious: Mos Espa's famous Podrace circuit now runs directly through the stones.

The activities of Tatooine's settlers disrupt the traditional hunting patterns of the indigenous Sand People. The result has been intense periods of frustrated savagery. These fearsome natives now attack other species in random raids, and take potshots using stolen blasters as weapons.

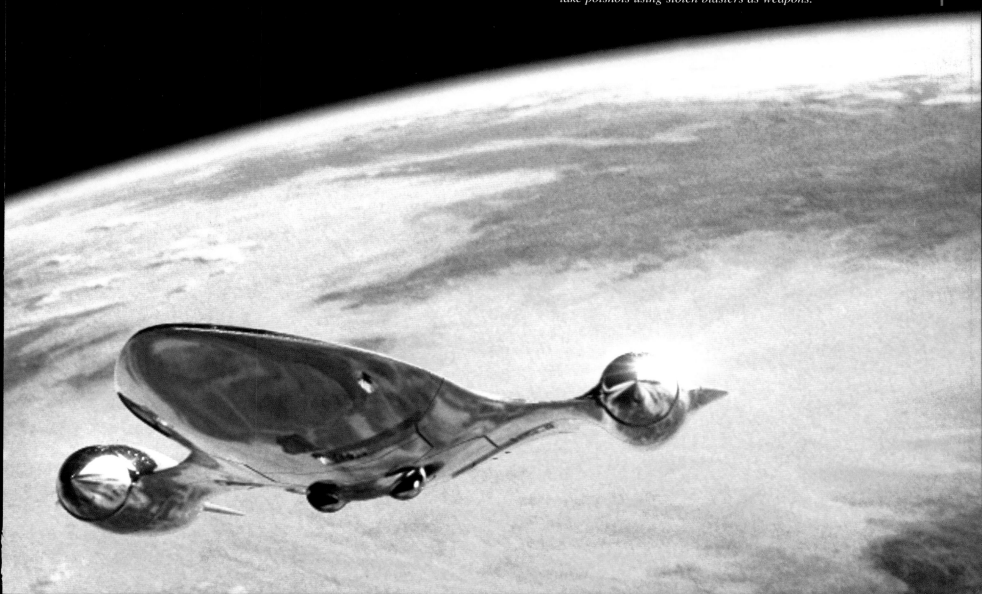

MOS ESPA

Inhabited mostly by poor settlers and controlled by powerful gangsters, Mos Espa is a rough, lawless town and one of Tatooine's largest spaceports. Its inhabitants eke out a living by scavenging, trading, stealing, or gambling. The wealthiest citizens openly disregard the Republic's laws by owning slaves, an illegal practice. Slaves are housed on the outskirts of Mos Espa in cheap lodgings originally put up by mining corporations for their workers. Since local authorities stay away from the slave quarters, enterprising slaves regularly provide safe houses for outlaws on the run—for a price.

Although the food is guaranteed to be undercooked and stringy, Sebulba often hangs out at Akim's Munch, a street café where his fans can see him and pay their respects. The hot-tempered Dug, however, is just as keen to meet opponents and enemies.

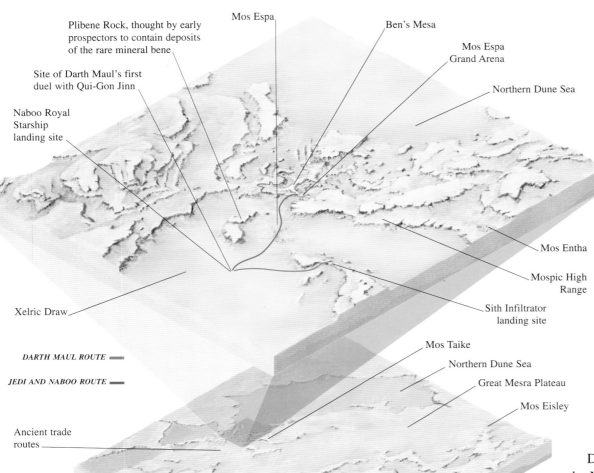

Plibene Rock, thought by early prospectors to contain deposits of the rare mineral bene

Mos Espa

Ben's Mesa

Mos Espa Grand Arena

Northern Dune Sea

Site of Darth Maul's first duel with Qui-Gon Jinn

Naboo Royal Starship landing site

Mos Entha

Mospic High Range

Xelric Draw

Sith Infiltrator landing site

DARTH MAUL ROUTE —

JEDI AND NABOO ROUTE —

Mos Taike

Northern Dune Sea

Great Mesra Plateau

Mos Eisley

Ancient trade routes

Fort Tusken

Jawa mountain fortress

Jundland Wastes

Western Dune Sea

Famous site of krayt dragon skeleton

DESERT SETTLEMENT

Mos Espa is strategically situated in the Xelric Draw, a shallow, wide-mouthed canyon that splits the Mospic High Range on the edge of the Northern Dune Sea. The Xelric Draw is an ancient trading route that links the northern settlements to those further south. Since all traders must pass this way, Mos Espa's marketplace developed quickly. Settlements off the main trade route tend to be even more lawless and hostile toward traders of any species.

HOVEL BACKYARDS

Anakin works on his Podracer behind the slave quarters safe in the knowledge that Watto never ventures here. As a slave owner, Watto is expected to maintain slave hovels. However, repairs are usually left undone until structures actually begin to collapse—then they are hastily patched up by one of Watto's most expendable droids.

MOS ESPA ARENA

Many off-worlders from the Outer Rim associate Mos Espa with its famous Podraces, held at the enormous arena in the desert outside the city. The thrill of the races can be addictive, and fans new to the sport soon find Tatooine-style gambling to be an expensive pursuit.

DESPERATE SELLING

Mos Espa's market stalls are busy with salvage dealers selling ill-gotten used parts for all manner of vehicles and vessels. An off-worlder who neglects to leave his ship under guard will almost certainly find parts missing on return!

URBAN MUDDLE

Mos Espa's domed, mostly windowless architecture is intended to protect settlers from the burning heat of Tatooine's suns—and from each other. With the absence of any discernible building codes, new streets and buildings are tacked on whenever needed. Shacks stand shoulder to shoulder with cupolas; vendors with over-head awnings do business next to climate-controlled trading houses. Only long-time residents are able to make their way through the labyrinth of dusty streets without a map—visitors are at a distinct disadvantage, and risk losing their way and their valuables at every turn.

CHANGING LANDSCAPES

Tatooine's cities are frequently blasted by severe sandstorms. The market vendors of Mos Espa seem to know instinctively when one is approaching. At the first sign, outdoor traders cover their wares with faded tarps while shopkeepers close their doors and plug vents. In a sandstorm, even seasoned inhabitants lose their way within city limits, mistaking one sandswept building for another. Adding to Tatooine's ever-changing landscapes are mirages and heat hazes: the dark cantinas are full of haunting stories of lost travelers and the desert apparitions they have seen.

WATTO'S JUNKSHOP

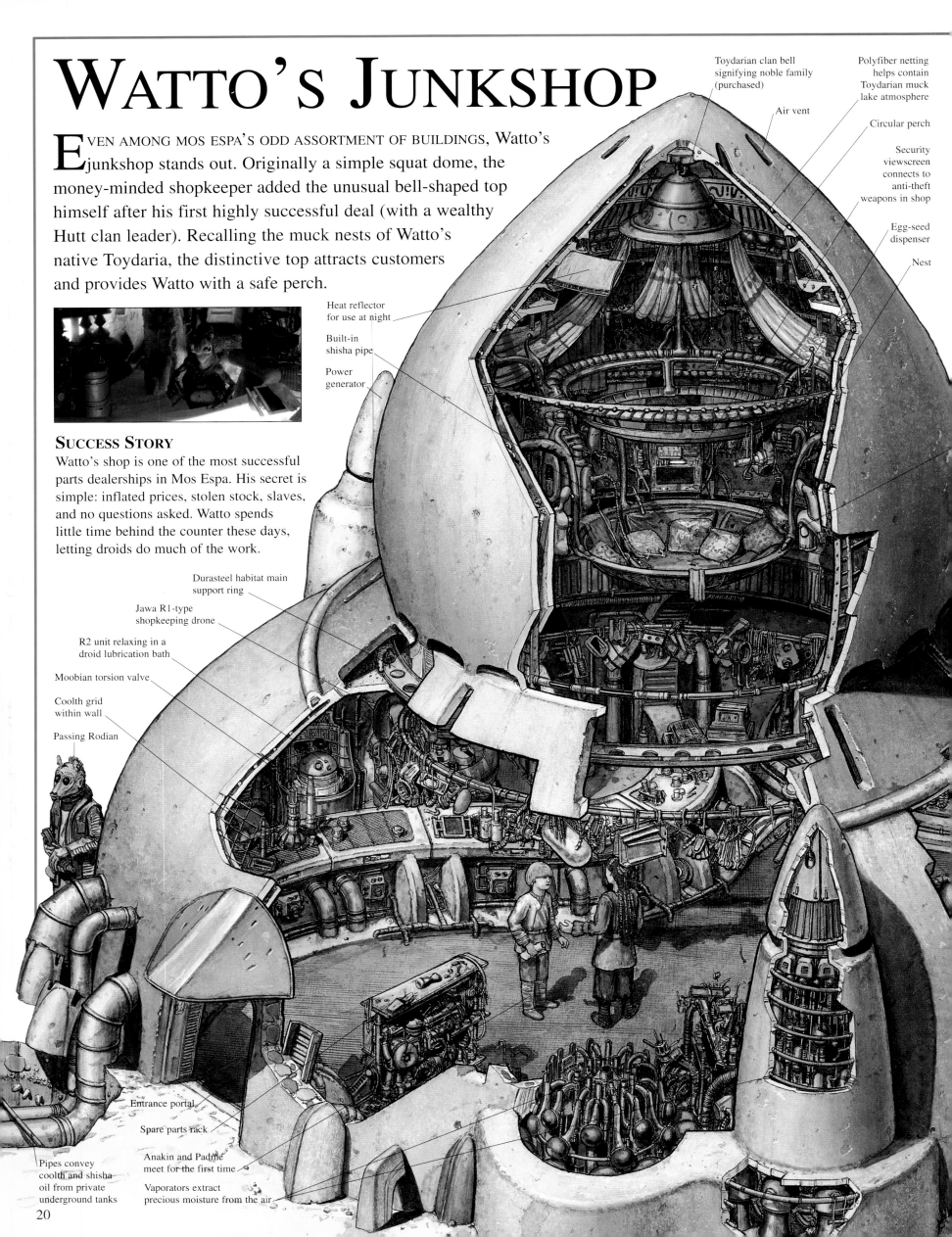

EVEN AMONG MOS ESPA'S ODD ASSORTMENT OF BUILDINGS, Watto's junkshop stands out. Originally a simple squat dome, the money-minded shopkeeper added the unusual bell-shaped top himself after his first highly successful deal (with a wealthy Hutt clan leader). Recalling the muck nests of Watto's native Toydaria, the distinctive top attracts customers and provides Watto with a safe perch.

SUCCESS STORY

Watto's shop is one of the most successful parts dealerships in Mos Espa. His secret is simple: inflated prices, stolen stock, slaves, and no questions asked. Watto spends little time behind the counter these days, letting droids do much of the work.

Toydarian clan bell signifying noble family (purchased)

Air vent

Polyfiber netting helps contain Toydarian muck lake atmosphere

Circular perch

Security viewscreen connects to anti-theft weapons in shop

Egg-seed dispenser

Nest

Heat reflector for use at night

Built-in shisha pipe

Power generator

Durasteel habitat main support ring

Jawa R1-type shopkeeping drone

R2 unit relaxing in a droid lubrication bath

Moobian torsion valve

Coolth grid within wall

Passing Rodian

Entrance portal

Spare parts rack

Pipes convey coolth and shisha oil from private underground tanks

Anakin and Padmé meet for the first time

Vaporators extract precious moisture from the air

ANAKIN'S WORKBENCH

When Anakin isn't repairing droids for Watto, he spends his precious spare time tinkering and inventing. He works on his Podracer engines outdoors due to their size. When it gets dark, Shmi calls Anakin inside and he works at his workbench on the protocol droid he is building for his mother.

Half-finished scanner Anakin is inventing to detect hidden slave implants

T3 web comber

C-3PO

Anti-static toolbox

Power coupler

Gausser (broken)

POWER FROM WASTE

Slave hovels on Tatooine are cooled and heated archaic bio-converter power generators. These machines receive liquid sludge composed of animal and munici waste via underground pipelin The liquid is then converted in natchgas. The Skywalkers' over-sized generator also serves four adjacent hovels.

Diagnostic screen

Storage cupboard fabricated from a gutted jukebox from Mos Espa's first cantina

Murchason ring stress analyzer

Anakin shows Padmé his room

Woven rug takes its pattern from rock paintings found in Tatooine's interior

Box left by previous tenant

Workbench

Bed alcove

Karmova drum

Noeu sphere racquets

Dried poonten grass bedding

Rough, poor-quality blankets on Anakin's bed

Thick adobe walls offer cool protection from Tatooine's harsh twin suns and fierce sandstorms

Stone infill mined locally at Ebe Crater quarry

ANAKIN'S ROOM

Filled with the clutter of an active nine-year-old's life, Anakin's bedroom houses his mechanical projects, spare parts, and tools, as well as his home-made toys and games.

Coolth in-flow pipe leading to second level of hovel

Clothing storage

R2-D2

Repulsor-operated door

Stairs to upper level and refresher

ANAKIN'S HOVEL

Anakin and Shmi Skywalker share a hovel in Slave Quarters Row on the edge of Mos Espa. They have been fortunate to have a home to themselves ever since Watto won them in a gambling debt from the fearsome Gardulla the Hutt. When the Skywalkers belonged to Gardulla, they were forced to share quarters with six other slaves. Their good fortune is not due to Watto's generosity, of course. He reluctantly lets them live alone until he can afford more slaves—a threat he uses against the Skywalkers whenever he is displeased with them.

The hovels are stacked on top of each other to save space.

MOS ESPA ARENA

THE IMMENSE GRANDSTANDS of Mos Espa Arena are cradled within a natural canyon amphitheater on the edge of the Western Dune Sea. Constructed of sandrock and ditanium over durasteel supports, the arena seats more than 100,000 fans—though many more squeeze in for major events like the Boonta Eve Classic. While high-priced tickets for Podraces are widely sold to gullible off-worlders, Tatooine's regulars simply turn up on speeders and push their way into the barely regulated stands.

FROM LOCAL CULT TO GRAND SPECTACLE

For a long time before the arena was built, Tatooine's thrill-seekers have held free-for-all, no-holds-barred races here, first on animal-drawn carts, then on hanno speeders (a precursor to the landspeeder), and, finally, on Podracers. The era of modern Podracing was instigated on Malastare by a fearless alien racer called Gustab Wenbus, who entered himself on a virtually untested, super-fast prototype Podracer that had been designed for him by a rogue mechanic called Phoebus. As use of these death-defying Podracers became standard, Podracing on Tatooine quickly began to draw fans from far across the space lanes.

History of Podracing exhibit

Race viewing gallery

Bo Charmian Racing School

Trophy Room

Holding cells for debtors

Gambling Hall

Arena employees watch race from roof

Coolth cells in domes ventilate buildings

Arena citadel with betting floors

Refreshment booths employ vendors to work the crowds

After a number of spectators died from overheating, floating canopies were put up in a bid to prevent further adverse publicity; in fact, the canopies give very little protection

Spectators constantly jostle each other for extra room on the overcrowded seats

Shaded seats reserved for children are generally appropriated by gangsters and bounty hunters

Security watchtowers

ROYAL BOX

With an entourage of aides, body guards, sycophants, and hangers-on, the wealthy gangster Jabba the Hutt presides over the Boonta Eve Classic from the best box seats in the arena. Podracing has proved a lucrative racket for Jabba; he financed the construction of the grandstands and makes an immense profit from controlling the betting. However, aside from his passion for gambling and crime, the races bore Jabba: his depraved senses are not stimulated by screaming, high-speed vehicles.

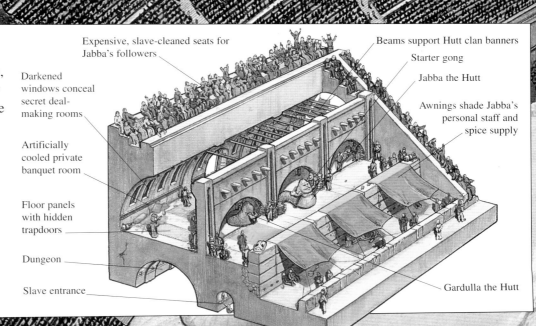

Expensive, slave-cleaned seats for Jabba's followers

Beams support Hutt clan banners

Starter gong

Jabba the Hutt

Awnings shade Jabba's personal staff and spice supply

Darkened windows conceal secret deal-making rooms

Artificially cooled private banquet room

Floor panels with hidden trapdoors

Dungeon

Slave entrance

Race officials' building

Starters' box

Gardulla the Hutt

Sebulba in first place

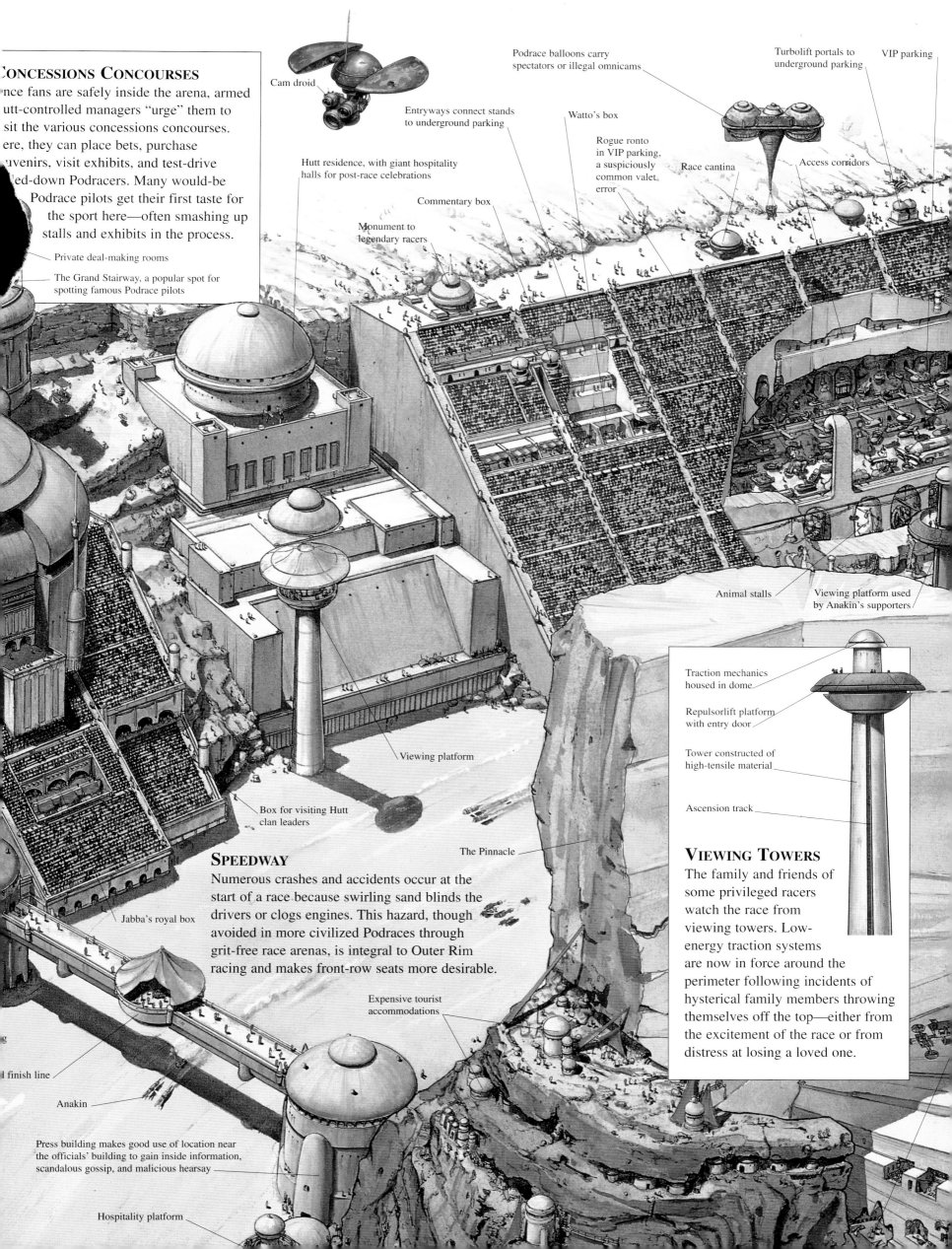

CONCESSIONS CONCOURSES

nce fans are safely inside the arena, armed
utt-controlled managers "urge" them to
sit the various concessions concourses.
ere, they can place bets, purchase
uvenirs, visit exhibits, and test-drive
ed-down Podracers. Many would-be
Podrace pilots get their first taste for
the sport here—often smashing up
stalls and exhibits in the process.

Private deal-making rooms

The Grand Stairway, a popular spot for
spotting famous Podrace pilots

Cam droid

Podrace balloons carry
spectators or illegal omnicams

Turbolift portals to
underground parking

VIP parking

Entryways connect stands
to underground parking

Watto's box

Hutt residence, with giant hospitality
halls for post-race celebrations

Rogue ronto
in VIP parking,
a suspiciously
common valet
error

Race cantina

Access corridors

Commentary box

Monument to
legendary racers

Animal stalls

Viewing platform used
by Anakin's supporters

Traction mechanics
housed in dome

Repulsorlift platform
with entry door

Tower constructed of
high-tensile material

Ascension track

Viewing platform

Box for visiting Hutt
clan leaders

The Pinnacle

VIEWING TOWERS

The family and friends of
some privileged racers
watch the race from
viewing towers. Low-
energy traction systems
are now in force around the
perimeter following incidents of
hysterical family members throwing
themselves off the top—either from
the excitement of the race or from
distress at losing a loved one.

SPEEDWAY

Numerous crashes and accidents occur at the
start of a race because swirling sand blinds the
drivers or clogs engines. This hazard, though
avoided in more civilized Podraces through
grit-free race arenas, is integral to Outer Rim
racing and makes front-row seats more desirable.

Jabba's royal box

Expensive tourist
accommodations

finish line

Anakin

Press building makes good use of location near
the officials' building to gain inside information,
scandalous gossip, and malicious hearsay

Hospitality platform

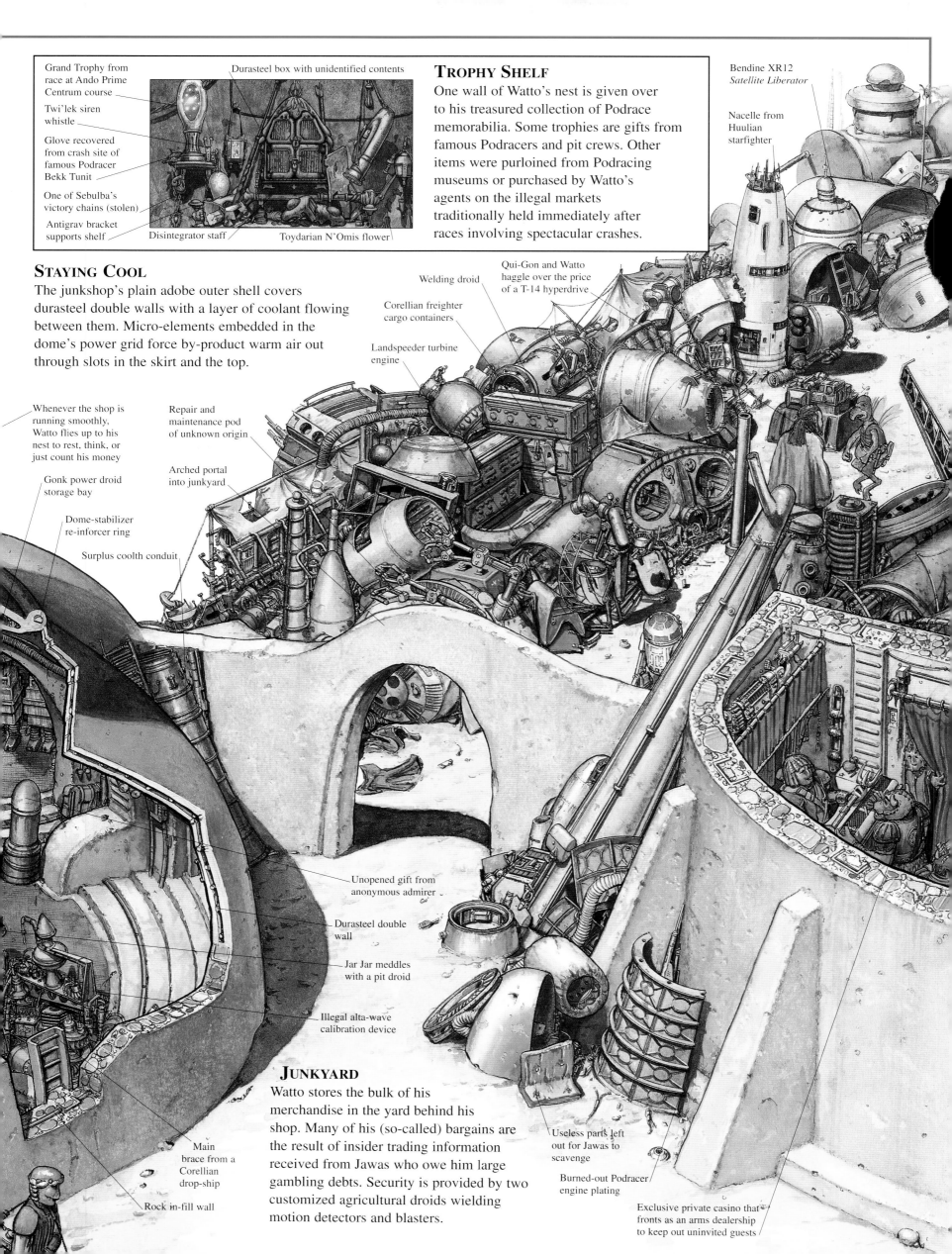

TROPHY SHELF

One wall of Watto's nest is given over to his treasured collection of Podrace memorabilia. Some trophies are gifts from famous Podracers and pit crews. Other items were purloined from Podracing museums or purchased by Watto's agents on the illegal markets traditionally held immediately after races involving spectacular crashes.

Grand Trophy from race at Ando Prime Centrum course

Twi'lek siren whistle

Glove recovered from crash site of famous Podracer Bekk Tunit

One of Sebulba's victory chains (stolen)

Antigrav bracket supports shelf

Durasteel box with unidentified contents

Disintegrator staff

Toydarian N'Omis flower

Bendine XR12 *Satellite Liberator*

Nacelle from Huulian starfighter

STAYING COOL

The junkshop's plain adobe outer shell covers durasteel double walls with a layer of coolant flowing between them. Micro-elements embedded in the dome's power grid force by-product warm air out through slots in the skirt and the top.

Whenever the shop is running smoothly, Watto flies up to his nest to rest, think, or just count his money

Gonk power droid storage bay

Dome-stabilizer re-inforcer ring

Surplus coolth conduit

Repair and maintenance pod of unknown origin

Arched portal into junkyard

Welding droid

Qui-Gon and Watto haggle over the price of a T-14 hyperdrive

Corellian freighter cargo containers

Landspeeder turbine engine

Unopened gift from anonymous admirer

Durasteel double wall

Jar Jar meddles with a pit droid

Illegal alta-wave calibration device

Main brace from a Corellian drop-ship

Rock in-fill wall

JUNKYARD

Watto stores the bulk of his merchandise in the yard behind his shop. Many of his (so-called) bargains are the result of insider trading information received from Jawas who owe him large gambling debts. Security is provided by two customized agricultural droids wielding motion detectors and blasters.

Useless parts left out for Jawas to scavenge

Burned-out Podracer engine plating

Exclusive private casino that fronts as an arms dealership to keep out uninvited guests

Sludge
intake duct

Bio-converter
power generator

Qui-Gon and Shmi
discuss Anakin's future

SLAVE QUARTERS

The hovels were built by the mining
companies that originally settled Tatooine.
Desiring cheap, temporary housing for
their workers, they piled arched,
windowless, adobe chambers on top of
one another. The only way to enter the
top levels is to climb up the outside
on uneven stone stairways.

Thermo-static cleaner (beneath panel)

Jar Jar Binks thinks about food

Heavily glazed louvered
windows diffuse the
harsh desert light

Thermic baster

Polta bean pan

Old-style bread
oven

Slave quarters
brazier

Upper story

Door entry
device

Main door into
hovel

Static sand-trap flooring

Shmi's workstation

Shmi's
bedroom

Sealed doors indicate that the Skywalkers'
home was once three smaller hovels

Sonic welder

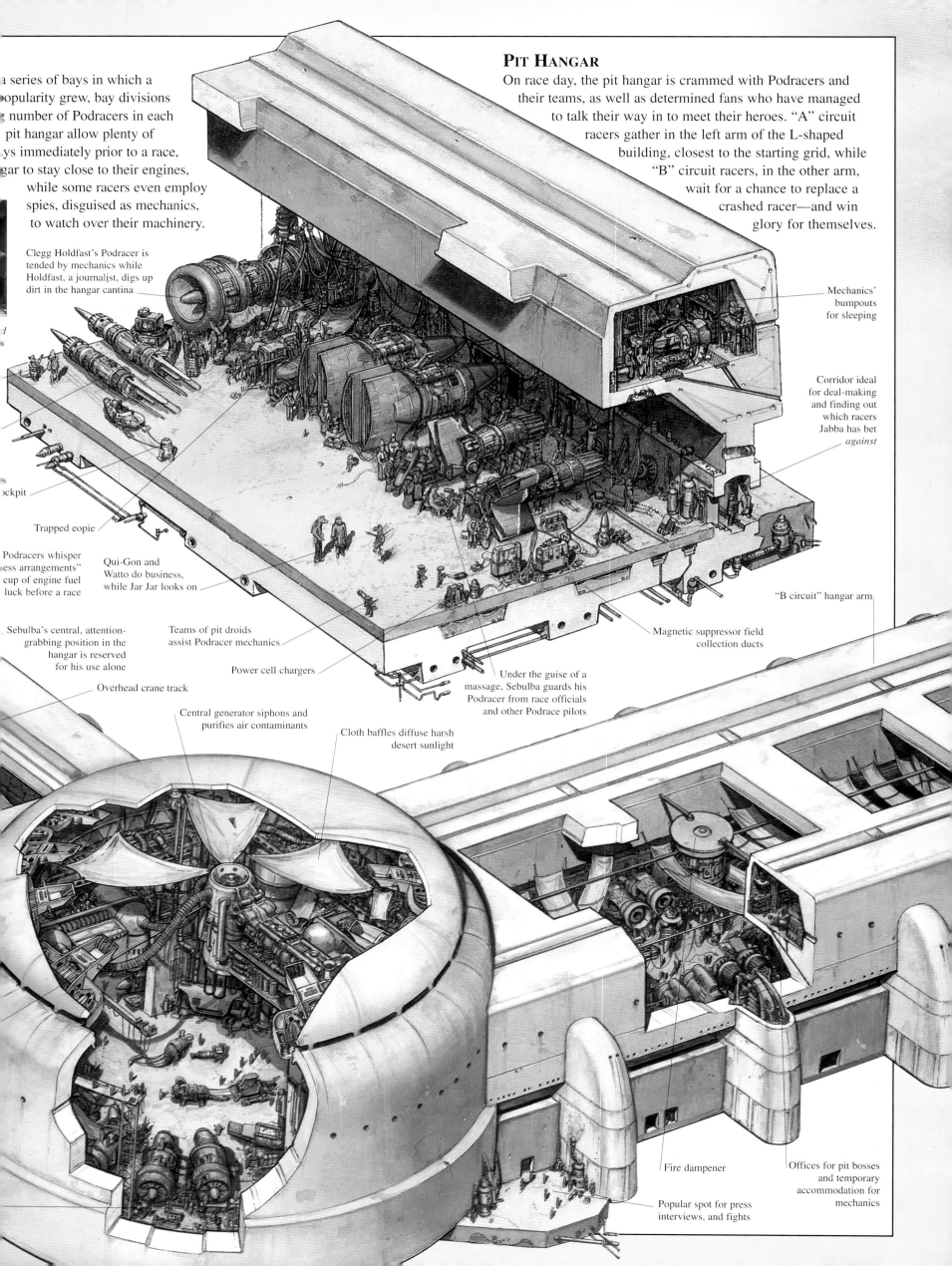

a series of bays in which a
...opularity grew, bay divisions
...g number of Podracers in each
... pit hangar allow plenty of
...ys immediately prior to a race,
...ar to stay close to their engines,
while some racers even employ
spies, disguised as mechanics,
to watch over their machinery.

PIT HANGAR

On race day, the pit hangar is crammed with Podracers and
their teams, as well as determined fans who have managed
to talk their way in to meet their heroes. "A" circuit
racers gather in the left arm of the L-shaped
building, closest to the starting grid, while
"B" circuit racers, in the other arm,
wait for a chance to replace a
crashed racer—and win
glory for themselves.

Clegg Holdfast's Podracer is
tended by mechanics while
Holdfast, a journalist, digs up
dirt in the hangar cantina

Mechanics'
bumpouts
for sleeping

Corridor ideal
for deal-making
and finding out
which racers
Jabba has bet
against

...ckpit

Trapped eopie

...Podracers whisper
...ess arrangements"
...cup of engine fuel
...luck before a race

Qui-Gon and
Watto do business,
while Jar Jar looks on

"B circuit" hangar arm

Sebulba's central, attention-
grabbing position in the
hangar is reserved
for his use alone

Teams of pit droids
assist Podracer mechanics

Magnetic suppressor field
collection ducts

Power cell chargers

Under the guise of a
massage, Sebulba guards his
Podracer from race officials
and other Podrace pilots

Overhead crane track

Central generator siphons and
purifies air contaminants

Cloth baffles diffuse harsh
desert sunlight

Fire dampener

Offices for pit bosses
and temporary
accommodation for
mechanics

Popular spot for press
interviews, and fights

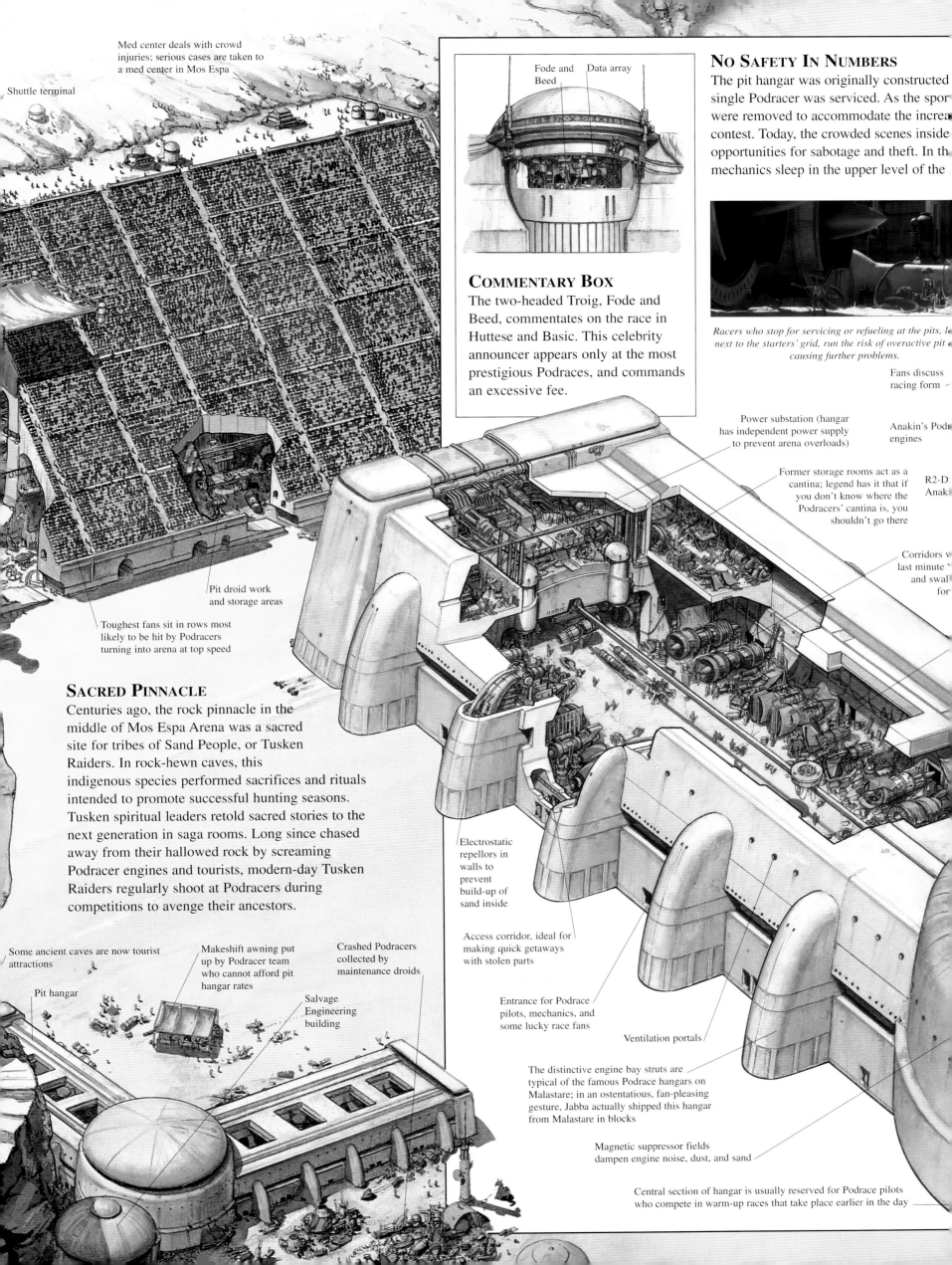

Med center deals with crowd injuries; serious cases are taken to a med center in Mos Espa

Shuttle terminal

Fode and Beed

Data array

COMMENTARY BOX
The two-headed Troig, Fode and Beed, commentates on the race in Huttese and Basic. This celebrity announcer appears only at the most prestigious Podraces, and commands an excessive fee.

NO SAFETY IN NUMBERS
The pit hangar was originally constructed single Podracer was serviced. As the spor were removed to accommodate the increa contest. Today, the crowded scenes inside opportunities for sabotage and theft. In th mechanics sleep in the upper level of the

Racers who stop for servicing or refueling at the pits, le next to the starters' grid, run the risk of overactive pit causing further problems.

Fans discuss racing form

Power substation (hangar has independent power supply to prevent arena overloads)

Anakin's Podr engines

Former storage rooms act as a cantina; legend has it that if you don't know where the Podracers' cantina is, you shouldn't go there

R2-D Anaki

Corridors w last minute and swal for

Pit droid work and storage areas

Toughest fans sit in rows most likely to be hit by Podracers turning into arena at top speed

SACRED PINNACLE
Centuries ago, the rock pinnacle in the middle of Mos Espa Arena was a sacred site for tribes of Sand People, or Tusken Raiders. In rock-hewn caves, this indigenous species performed sacrifices and rituals intended to promote successful hunting seasons. Tusken spiritual leaders retold sacred stories to the next generation in saga rooms. Long since chased away from their hallowed rock by screaming Podracer engines and tourists, modern-day Tusken Raiders regularly shoot at Podracers during competitions to avenge their ancestors.

Some ancient caves are now tourist attractions

Pit hangar

Makeshift awning put up by Podracer team who cannot afford pit hangar rates

Crashed Podracers collected by maintenance droids

Salvage Engineering building

Electrostatic repellors in walls to prevent build-up of sand inside

Access corridor, ideal for making quick getaways with stolen parts

Entrance for Podrace pilots, mechanics, and some lucky race fans

Ventilation portals

The distinctive engine bay struts are typical of the famous Podrace hangars on Malastare; in an ostentatious, fan-pleasing gesture, Jabba actually shipped this hangar from Malastare in blocks

Magnetic suppressor fields dampen engine noise, dust, and sand

Central section of hangar is usually reserved for Podrace pilots who compete in warm-up races that take place earlier in the day

MOS ESPA CIRCUIT

Host to the eagerly awaited Boonta Eve Classic and countless other races, Mos Espa Podrace circuit weaves around a broad, flat-topped mountain called Ben's Mesa. Its cliff-like sides help ensure that scheming racers stick to the official course. Nevertheless, pilots continue to experiment with new fast-cuts through the desert wilderness—no pilot or fan has ever agreed which route guarantees a spectacular win.

2 Ben Quadinaros is one of many pilots who stall on the starting grid. Usually, they are moved quickly to avoid collision with pilots returning at the end of lap one. In Ben's case, however, his Podracer explodes before pit droids can get to him.

BEGGAR'S CANYON

On non-race days, Tatooine youngsters sneak into the section of the course known as Beggar's Canyon. Here, in the winding channels of this dry river bed, they push their souped-up landspeeders and super-fast skyhoppers to the limit, dreaming that one day they might be hometown heroes.

Service ramps provide race personnel with access to valley floors when they need to scavenge for parts or make occasional repairs to cam droids

The small houses in Beggar's Canyon are inhabited by hermits who were chased out of Mos Espa ... and bounty hunters on the run

The sudden drop into Ebe Crater Valley causes many crashes; in the third lap, Sebulba bumps the ground but quickly regains control

Lesser races than the Boonta Eve avoid the perilous Arch Canyon, routing pilots over the Dune Sea instead

Map labels: Dead Man's Turn, Diablo Cut, Beggar's Canyon, Stone Needle, The Notch, MUSHROOM MESA, EBE CRATER VALLEY, DESERT PLAIN, DUNE SEA, BEN'S, The Whip, Gorge

3 Total concentration is needed in Mushroom Mesa, where shadows and harsh sunlight play tricks on pilots' depth perception. Mawhonic's dreams of winning are dashed when he focuses on his competitors rather than the course in lap one.

4 No pilot has managed to race up the steep gradient of a service ramp, keep control of the machine as it flips beyond its maximum repulsorlift altitude, and descend safely further along the circuit. Yet Anakin makes Podrace history by doing just this.

5 For Jawas, Podraces are fabulous scavenging opportunities. These cloaked Tatooine natives work in teams to cover as much of the circuit as possible, competing with P-100 Salvage Droids to pick up scrap engine parts from crash sites.

6 Sebulba treats the long, flat Desert Plain as light relief from the more demanding and difficult sections of the circuit. Inevitably, it is here that his vile mind turns to dirty tricks—and here that he brings down Mars Guo in the second lap.

7 In lap one, Ratts Tyerell crashes into a stalactite in Laguna Caves. Even if he had survived, he could have expected no help from rescue teams, who avoid the caves from fear of the krayt dragon that inhabits them.

1	ANAKIN SKYWALKER (Tatooine)	Time 15.42:655 (average speed 536 mph/858 kph)
2	GASGANO (Troiken)	Time 15.48:557 (average speed 531 mph/850 kph)
3	ALDAR BEEDO (Ploo II)	Time 15.52:108 (average speed 528 mph/845 kph)
4	EBE ENDOCOTT (Triffis)	Time 16.04:994 (average speed 517 mph/827 kph)
5	ELAN MAK (Ploo IV)	Time 16.10:737 (average speed 512 mph/819 kph)
6	BOLES ROOR (Sneeve)	Time 16.42:473 (average speed 488 mph/781 kph)
7	CLEGG HOLDFAST (New Plympto)	Time 28.55:581 (average speed 270 mph/432 kph)
X	BEN QUADINAROS (Toong System)	No laps Engine stalled at start
X	MAWHONIC (Hok)	Lap 1 Crashed in Mushroom Mesa
X	RATTS TYERELL (Aleen)	Lap 1 Accelerator jammed in Laguna Caves
X	ODY MANDRELL (Tatooine)	Lap 2 Engine burned out on circuit after pit stop
X	NEVA KEE (Xagobah)	Lap 2 Leaves circuit at Hutt Flats (still missing)
X	MARS GUO (Phu)	Lap 2 Crashed in Desert Plain (suspected sabotage)
X	TEEMTO PAGALIES (Moonus Mandel)	Lap 2 Vaporized in Canyon Dune Turn
X	WAN SANDAGE (Ord Radama)	Lap 3 Collided with Jawa sandcrawler off-course
X	DUD BOLT (Vulpter)	Lap 3 Collided with Ark Roose in The Coil
X	ARK "BUMPY" ROOSE (Sump)	Lap 3 Collided with Dud Bolt in The Coil
X	SEBULBA (Malastare)	Lap 3 Crashed in Hutt Flats

— Race circuit
--- Underground section

0   500 ft
0   150 m

MOS ESPA ARENA

1 When the Podrace pilots line up on the starting grid, the crowd erupts with a deafening roar. This is the last chance for thousands of gamblers to size up the pilots and their Podracers before placing their final bets.

Seasoned racers have come to believe that the faces that can be discerned in the stones of Mushroom Mesa change expressions when viewed from different angles

WALDO FLATS

Waldo Grade

MESA

Ben's Mesa, named after Ben Neluenf, the first great Tatooine-born racer, who lost his life in a spectacular attempt to scale the central mesa

Laguna Caves

STARLITE FLATS

Bindy Bend

Pilots are forced to keep to the outside of the large stone spindle as they make the turn around Bindy Bend; the jagged rocks on the nearside are not worth risking

The Coil

Canyon Dune Turn

Hutt Flats is the bed of prehistoric Lake Anre, which once ran to the Northern Dune Sea via underground tributaries

HUTT FLATS

11 The final section of the circuit, Hutt Flats, brings out the worst behavior in pilots. Accelerating to top speed, it is their last chance before the finish line to fight for position. This time, however, it is Sebulba who is blown out of the race.

Pilots must flip their vehicles on their sides to pass through Devil's Doorknob

The Corkscrew

Jett's Chute

10 In the final lap, the dastardly Sebulba attempts to force Anakin out of the race using the sheer weight and size of his massive Podracer. It is a tactic he has used in the past to crowd-pleasing effect.

Repulsorlift

Re-grav plates in holding arm carry as much as 500 kg (1,100 lb) of scrap

Omnidirectional homing mechanics locate distress beacons in downed Podracers

Hold stores three pick-up droids with legs folded

Pick-up droid released from underside of P-100

The mechanic who worked on this Podracer before the race removes his own "unique modifications"

CRASH CLEAN-UP
Before the dust even settles around a crashed Podracer, P-100 Salvage Droids arrive to remove the valuable parts. Pilots have just two hours to claim their junked vehicles before they are auctioned off or sold, usually to Jawas.

Remote pick-up droid transports crash debris to holding arm

8 In lap two, Teemto Pagalies is hit by Sand People taking pot shots from the cliffs above Canyon Dune Turn. Anonymous complaints by pilots to race officials have come to nothing as the Sand People's troublemaking has become a popular attraction!

9 In lap three, Anakin's engines overheat in Jett's Chute. A seriously hazardous section of the circuit, spectators come to blows over which strategy is faster—weaving in and out of the arches or "threading the needle" (slipping right through them).

CORUSCANT

CAPITAL OF THE REPUBLIC, seat of government, and home of the powerful Jedi Knights, Coruscant is the most important planet in the galaxy. One of the original Core Worlds that grouped together at the birth of the Republic, Coruscant distinguished itself with the development and production of hyperdrive mechanics. This is the single most important invention in the galaxy's history because it allowed ships to travel from one end of space to the other in a matter of days rather than years. As galactic scouts explored increasingly farflung planets, large numbers of alien species made the return trip to Coruscant, swelling its population and causing the most rapid expansion a planet had ever seen. Coruscant reaped the glory and was awarded the coordinates zero-zero-zero on standard navigation charts, making it the effective center of the Republic: whoever rules Coruscant is truly master of the galaxy.

CITY SKYLINE

Coruscant's dazzling skyline is a potent symbol of the power and authority concentrated in the city. Many of its buildings reach 6,000 meters (20,000 feet) into the atmosphere, with sleek, transparisteel edifices standing next to older duracrete structures. Negotiating a landing path through these towering skyscrapers is not a task for the fainthearted. Tour operator pilots demand high fees for taking wide-eyed offworlders on breathtaking cruises over the planet surface. Coruscant's air traffic is constant and busy, with large passenger ships traveling along autonavigated skylanes and smaller air taxis crisscrossing these routes to take high-paying passengers directly to their destinations.

JEDI TEMPLE

Below the towers of the Jedi Temple, Galactic City is a dense sprawl sliced through with deep, canyon-like thoroughfares. The Temple itself is reached via a long, broad promenade, which provides a symbolic and physical transition from urban tumult to Jedi tranquility. The Temple's serene exterior hides a more pragmatic interior, with many hundreds of rooms where the Jedi train, practice, meditate, and debate the problems of the Republic. The most sacred part of the building is the central tower, or Temple Spire, in which the original manuscripts of the founding Jedi are housed.

GALACTIC SENATE

The Galactic Senate stands out at the heart of Coruscant's densely packed government district. Here, thousands of elected senators represent their worlds in a vast, arena-like chamber. Statues adorning the entrance concourse depict the Republic's Core World founders. As the Senate swelled over time with representatives of a bewildering variety of intelligent life, the point is occasionally raised that the Core Worlds' humanoid statues are no longer characteristic of the present-day, multi-species Republic.

GALACTIC CITY

More than 12 billion individuals of diverse species live in
Galactic City, the most overpopulated, multifarious megatropolis
in the galaxy. Most of them aspire to work for the institutions of
galactic government. Yet for many, life on Coruscant is a room in a
low-level sector with artificial light and air, anonymous neighbors of
unknown species, and a data-input job in a government sub-office. In this
fast-paced, artificial world, few focus on anything outside their own
ambitions. Now the institutions of government are in decline, with
corruption, nepotism, and negligence decaying the Republic's ideals.

*Seen from space, Galactic City's brilliance is only slightly dimmed by
the planet's hazy cloud cover. Weather patterns are affected by the
troposphere-piercing buildings that cover the planet surface. Inside the
tallest buildings, enormous differences of temperature and air pressure
from bottom to top produce unusual and unpredictable micro-climates.*

SENATE APARTMENTS
Senator Palpatine resides
in one of Coruscant's
prestigious older districts.
Inhabited by citizens of
incredible wealth (and
some fame) who demand
and receive complete
privacy, *500 Republica*
offers private turbolifts and
clandestine security
armaments. The building's
stepped design
incorporates 53 skydocks
and can accomodate even
the largest air taxis as well
as private vessels.

MULTILEVELED CITY
The skyscrapers of Galactic City cover the entire planet
surface, dwarfing all the original natural features,
including mountains and (now dry) seas, which lie
somewhere in the depths. Lower floors have been
abandoned to mutant species and fearsome scavengers.

SENATE LANDING PLATFORMS
Private repulsorlift landing platforms can be reserved
for the thousands of sectorial representatives, aides,
and visiting dignitaries who arrive and depart daily on
Coruscant. Other visitors must make do with municipal
landing platforms, which are many kilometers wide
and usually severely overcrowded. Vehicles are
routinely forced to maintain a holding pattern for
several hours until a landing spot becomes available.

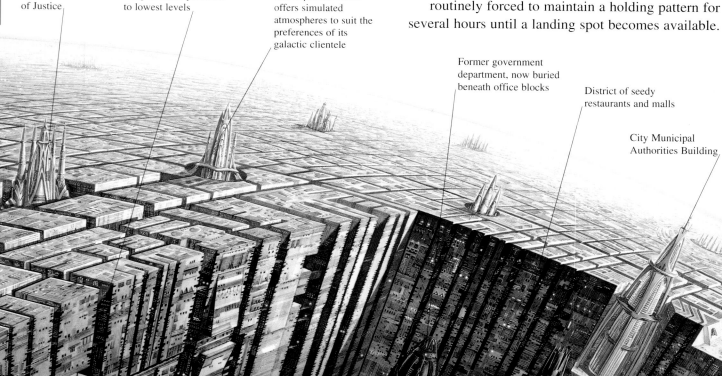

Galactic Courts
of Justice

Deep avenues penetrate
to lowest levels

The *Diplomat Hotel*
offers simulated
atmospheres to suit the
preferences of its
galactic clientele

Former government
department, now buried
beneath office blocks

District of seedy
restaurants and malls

City Municipal
Authorities Building

ATMOSPHERES

In the top levels of Galactic City, the richest citizens breathe their preferred choice of gas in high-grade, purified form. Their buildings are routinely scanned for impurities, and problems are dealt with by teams of quality-control droids. In the dirty underworld of tunnels and corridors at the base of the massive buildings, inhabitants struggle to exist on barely breathable combinations of waste gases. Many regular visitors to Coruscant choose to bring their own air supply to last the length of their stay.

PALPATINE'S GUEST APARTMENTS

When Queen Amidala travels to Galactic City, Senator Palpatine insists that she and her retinue stay in apartments in his own building. The expansive suite of rooms is thoughtfully decorated in Palpatine's preferred colors and fitted with remote bugging devices to ensure the complete safety of its regal guest during her stay. Armed guards at the door have been instructed to keep Palpatine fully informed of the Queen's every move.

CLANDESTINE MEETINGS

The architecture of Galactic City is ideally suited to the duplicitous machinations of the political classes that inhabit it. Hidden in the shadows and winding corridors of the megastructures are innumerable balconies, secret rooms, and abandoned buildings, many of which are used by clandestine organizations. In the anonymity afforded by this immense labyrinth, Darth Maul meets with his shadowy mentor, Darth Sidious, on a balcony, unnoticed by the teeming metropolis around them.

GALACTIC SENATE

THE GALACTIC SENATE BUILDING replaces a smaller, more intimate debating chamber instituted in the earliest days of the Republic. Reflecting the success of the expanding Republic, the enormous domed exterior of the modern structure is two kilometers (1.25 miles) in diameter. Inside, the debating rotunda accommodates platforms for more than 1,000 senators who represent the member worlds. The building's internal dynamics are designed to aid efficiency and the speed of decision-making. In fact, the convoluted network of private turbolifts and secret inner sanctums invites misuse, serving to facilitate underhanded dealmaking and avoidance of public accountability.

Receiving no natural light or air, the artificial atmosphere and illumination of the Senate's Great Rotunda is regulated to diminish senators' sense of time. This is intended to allow important debates to continue without being affected by nightfall.

CHANCELLOR'S PODIUM

The focus of the entire senate rotunda, the Supreme Chancellor's 30-meter (100-foot) tall podium is symbolic of both authority and, increasingly, vulnerability. Valorum and his staff are transported to the top by dedicated repulsorlift platforms that dock at the base of the podium. The Chancellor's extensive offices lie beneath the rotunda.

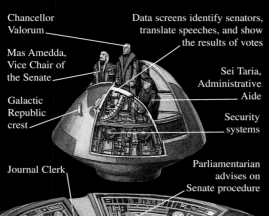

Chancellor Valorum

Mas Amedda, Vice Chair of the Senate

Galactic Republic crest

Journal Clerk

Data screens identify senators, translate speeches, and show the results of votes

Sei Taria, Administrative Aide

Security systems

Parliamentarian advises on Senate procedure

Sergeant-at-Arms supervises message droids, pages, and other Senate workers

Official Reporter records the verbatim proceedings of the Senate

Laser transmitters control information flow between podium and senatorial platforms

SENATORIAL BUSINESS

The Senate is responsible for creating laws, regulating commerce, mediating disputes, and making treaties. Decision-making is increasingly affected by powerful business interests such as the Trade Federation.

Quarren senator

Blast doors illustrate Neimoidian distrust of others

Alarmed anti-saboteur mesh between floors

Control room for senatorial platforms

Mechno-chair used by high-ranking Neimoidians

Intelligent mollusc keeps records

Atmosphere-regulated meeting rooms allow Dorins to move about freely without their breathing equipment

Artificial atmosphere generator

Hologram of Neimoidian Trade Monarch

Bubble-enclosed Dorin conference room

Imported luminescent and aromatic coral vegetation

Heavy water pools mimic deep water habitat

Platform used by senator for Kashyyyk

Turbolift transports senatorial guards to area behind senatorial platform (guards never enter a senator's chamber)

Specially constructed wall cavities in Neimoidian offices are filled with covert listening and recording devices

Wroshyr-wood cones imported from Kashyyyk

In-wall climate control

Venerated Wookiee elders take meetings while seated on cushions in wroshyr-paneled antechamber

Napping rooms promote longevity and strength

While drones take care of nearly all the Neimoidian delegation's work, aides and employees spend their work hours attending to the senator's needs

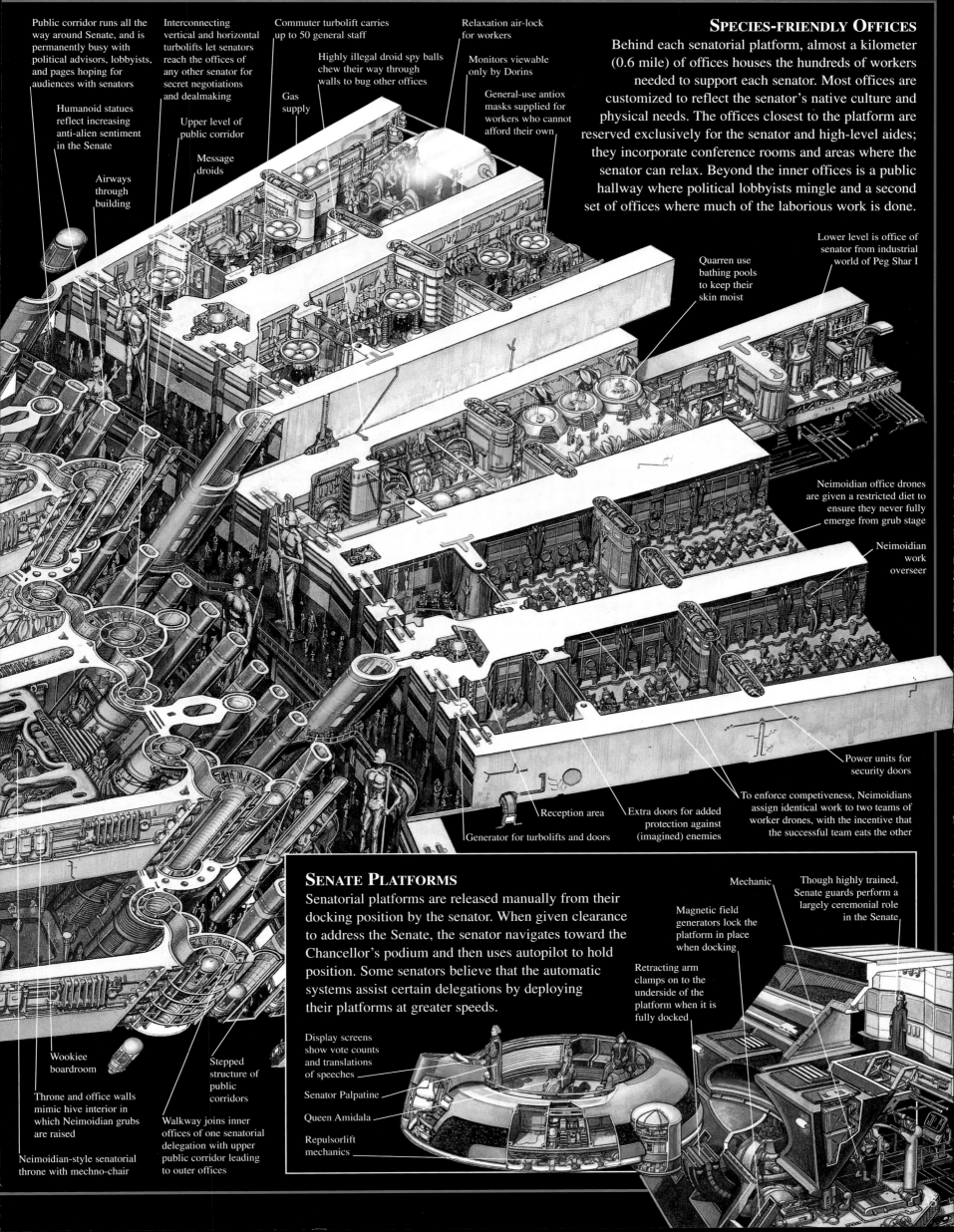

Public corridor runs all the way around Senate, and is permanently busy with political advisors, lobbyists, and pages hoping for audiences with senators

Humanoid statues reflect increasing anti-alien sentiment in the Senate

Airways through building

Interconnecting vertical and horizontal turbolifts let senators reach the offices of any other senator for secret negotiations and dealmaking

Upper level of public corridor

Message droids

Commuter turbolift carries up to 50 general staff

Highly illegal droid spy balls chew their way through walls to bug other offices

Gas supply

Relaxation air-lock for workers

Monitors viewable only by Dorins

General-use antiox masks supplied for workers who cannot afford their own

SPECIES-FRIENDLY OFFICES

Behind each senatorial platform, almost a kilometer (0.6 mile) of offices houses the hundreds of workers needed to support each senator. Most offices are customized to reflect the senator's native culture and physical needs. The offices closest to the platform are reserved exclusively for the senator and high-level aides; they incorporate conference rooms and areas where the senator can relax. Beyond the inner offices is a public hallway where political lobbyists mingle and a second set of offices where much of the laborious work is done.

Quarren use bathing pools to keep their skin moist

Lower level is office of senator from industrial world of Peg Shar I

Neimoidian office drones are given a restricted diet to ensure they never fully emerge from grub stage

Neimoidian work overseer

Power units for security doors

To enforce competiveness, Neimoidians assign identical work to two teams of worker drones, with the incentive that the successful team eats the other

Reception area

Extra doors for added protection against (imagined) enemies

Generator for turbolifts and doors

SENATE PLATFORMS

Senatorial platforms are released manually from their docking position by the senator. When given clearance to address the Senate, the senator navigates toward the Chancellor's podium and then uses autopilot to hold position. Some senators believe that the automatic systems assist certain delegations by deploying their platforms at greater speeds.

Mechanic

Though highly trained, Senate guards perform a largely ceremonial role in the Senate

Magnetic field generators lock the platform in place when docking

Retracting arm clamps on to the underside of the platform when it is fully docked

Display screens show vote counts and translations of speeches

Senator Palpatine

Queen Amidala

Repulsorlift mechanics

Wookiee boardroom

Throne and office walls mimic hive interior in which Neimoidian grubs are raised

Neimoidian-style senatorial throne with mechno-chair

Stepped structure of public corridors

Walkway joins inner offices of one senatorial delegation with upper public corridor leading to outer offices

JEDI TEMPLE

RISING ABOVE A LOW-RISE SECTOR of Galactic City to a height of a kilometer (0.6 mile), the Jedi Temple is the focus of Jedi life, the place where Jedi Knights are trained and housed. Its unobstructed position is not mere show, but a necessary aspect of its function. The five towers are each topped by powerful reception/transmission antennas, which use a wide range of broadcast-systems, the most sophisticated of which tap into the cosmic energy fields of the galaxy itself. Isolated by its height from the teeming city's electromagnetic fields, the towers' powerful communications array maintains contact with Jedi on far-flung missions.

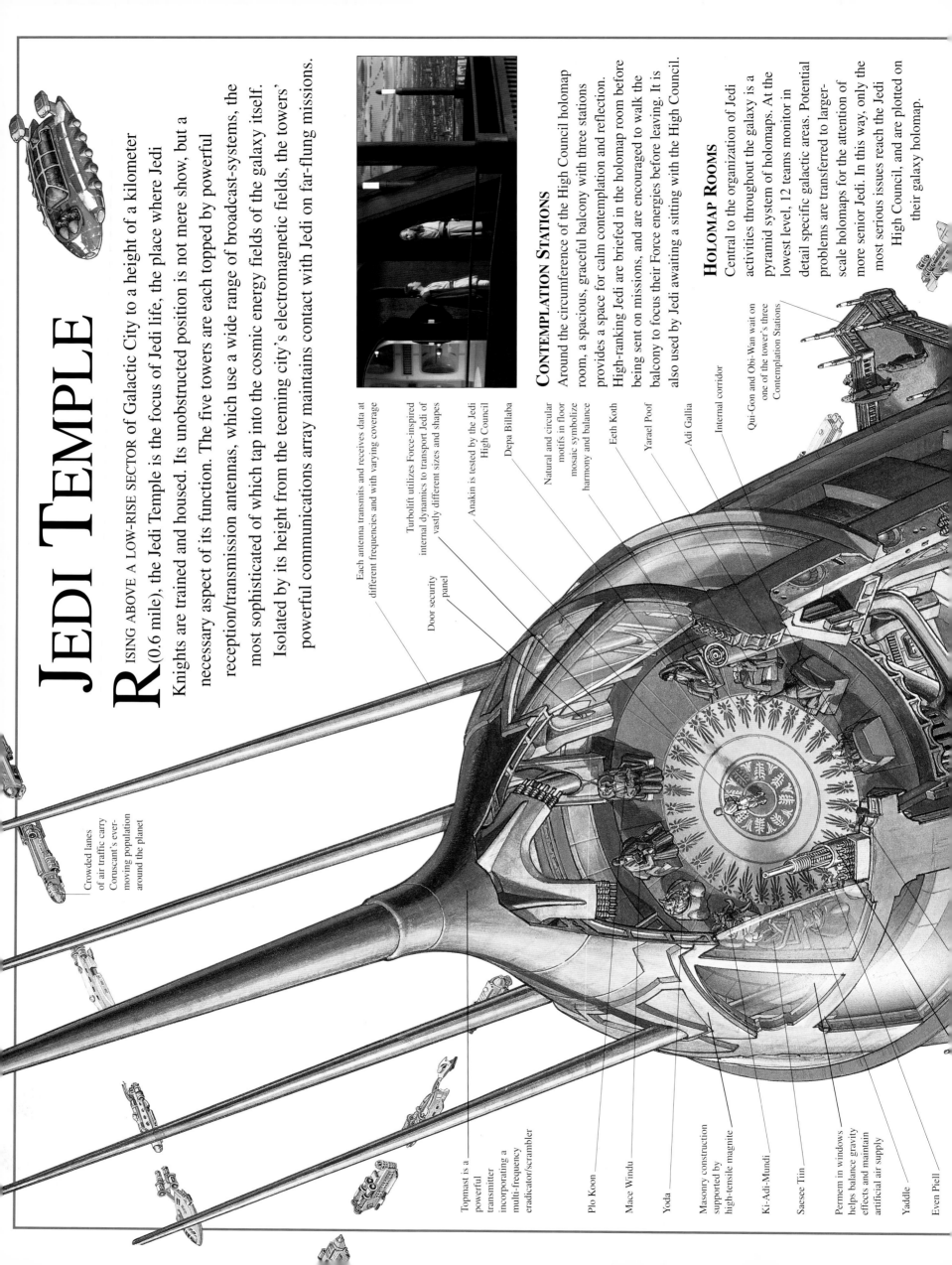

CONTEMPLATION STATIONS

Around the circumference of the High Council holomap room, a spacious, graceful balcony with three stations provides a space for calm contemplation and reflection. High-ranking Jedi are briefed in the holomap room before being sent on missions, and are encouraged to walk the balcony to focus their Force energies before leaving. It is also used by Jedi awaiting a sitting with the High Council.

HOLOMAP ROOMS

Central to the organization of Jedi activities throughout the galaxy is a pyramid system of holomaps. At the lowest level, 12 teams monitor in detail specific galactic areas. Potential problems are transferred to larger-scale holomaps for the attention of more senior Jedi. In this way, only the most serious issues reach the Jedi High Council, and are plotted on their galaxy holomap.

Each antenna transmits and receives data at different frequencies and with varying coverage

Turbolift utilizes Force-inspired internal dynamics to transport Jedi of vastly different sizes and shapes

Door security panel

Anakin is tested by the Jedi High Council

Depa Billaba

Natural and circular motifs in floor mosaic symbolize harmony and balance

Eeth Koth

Yarael Poof

Adi Gallia

Internal corridor

Qui-Gon and Obi-Wan wait on one of the tower's three Contemplation Stations

Crowded lanes of air traffic carry Coruscant's ever-moving population around the planet

Topmast is a powerful transmitter incorporating a multi-frequency eradicator/scrambler

Plo Koon

Mace Windu

Yoda

Masonry construction supported by high-tensile magnite

Permem in windows helps balance gravity effects and maintain artificial air supply

Saesee Tiin

Ki-Adi-Mundi

Yaddle

Even Piell

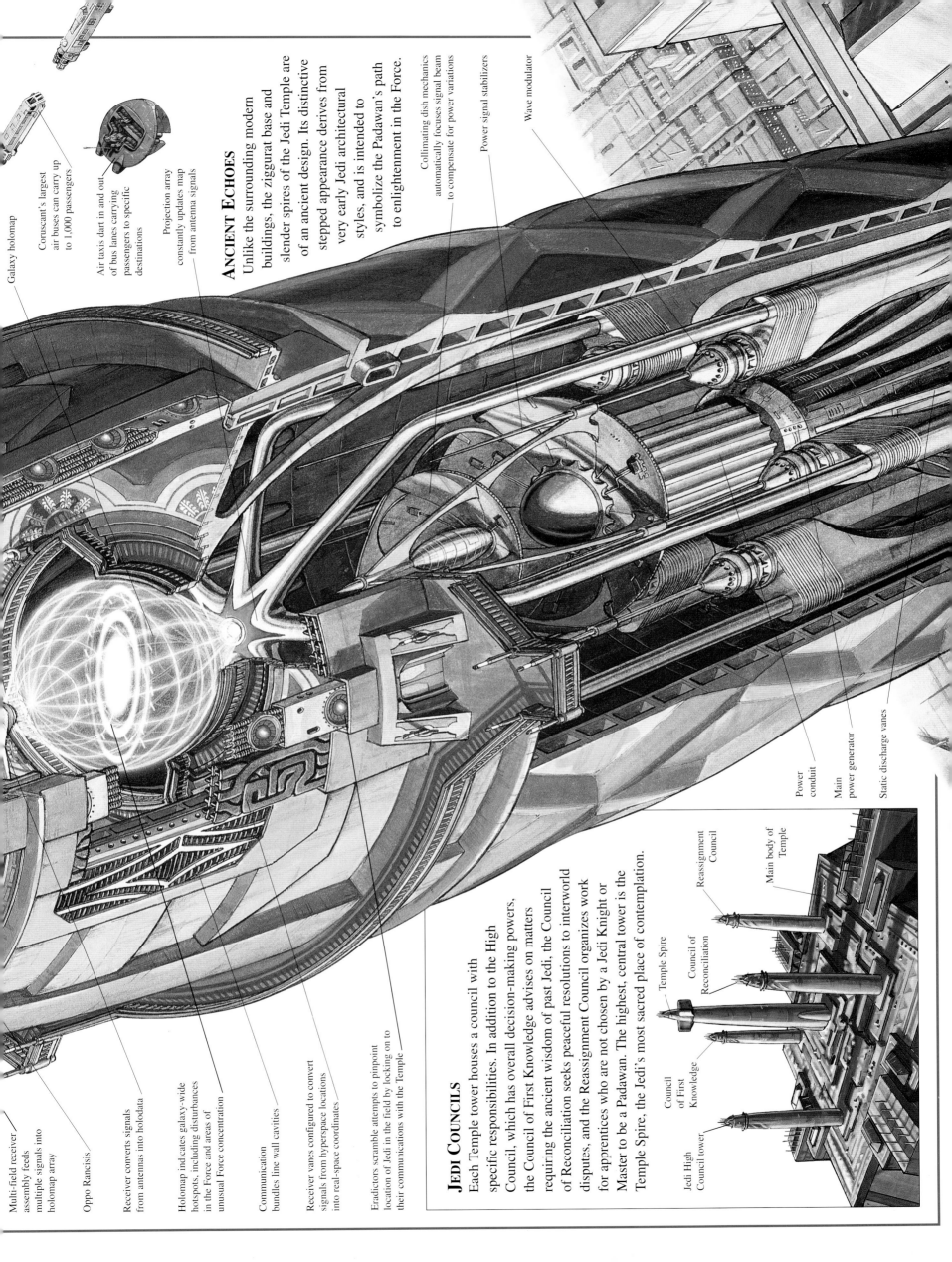

Galaxy holomap

Coruscant's largest air buses can carry up to 1,000 passengers

Air taxis dart in and out of bus lanes carrying passengers to specific destinations

Projection array constantly updates map from antenna signals

ANCIENT ECHOES

Unlike the surrounding modern buildings, the ziggurat base and slender spires of the Jedi Temple are of an ancient design. Its distinctive stepped appearance derives from very early Jedi architectural styles, and is intended to symbolize the Padawan's path to enlightenment in the Force.

Collimating dish mechanics automatically focuses signal beam to compensate for power variations

Power signal stabilizers

Wave modulator

Multi-field receiver assembly feeds multiple signals into holomap array

Oppo Rancisis

Receiver converts signals from antennas into holodata

Holomap indicates galaxy-wide hotspots, including disturbances in the Force and areas of unusual Force concentration

Communication bundles line wall cavities

Receiver vanes configured to convert signals from hyperspace locations into real-space coordinates

Eradictors scramble attempts to pinpoint location of Jedi in the field by locking on to their communications with the Temple

Power conduit

Main power generator

Static discharge vanes

JEDI COUNCILS

Each Temple tower houses a council with specific responsibilities. In addition to the High Council, which has overall decision-making powers, the Council of First Knowledge advises on matters requiring the ancient wisdom of past Jedi, the Council of Reconciliation seeks peaceful resolutions to interworld disputes, and the Reassignment Council organizes work for apprentices who are not chosen by a Jedi Knight or Master to be a Padawan. The highest, central tower is the Temple Spire, the Jedi's most sacred place of contemplation.

Reassignment Council

Main body of Temple

Temple Spire

Council of First Knowledge

Council of Reconciliation

Jedi High Council tower

THE INVASION OF NABOO

EVEN WHILE THE TRADE FEDERATION BLOCKADES NABOO with a fleet of war freighters, its leaders finalize invasion plans with their shadowy Sith mentor. The Neimoidians do not share Sidious' sinister interest in this small, relatively insignificant planet. However, they are persuaded that their victory will be easy—and ultimately profitable. On Sidious' orders, the invasion army has two primary objectives. The first is to sever Naboo's communication with the Senate. The second is to capture Queen Amidala and force her to sign a capitulation treaty. Sleek landing ships descend upon on the planet, avoiding public commotion by sticking to remote areas. Under cover of darkness, the army mobilizes and takes up strategic positions. The next morning, the citizens of Theed are caught unaware by a devastating surprise attack.

LANDING SHIPS

Formations of massive C-9979 landing ships descend like vultures through Naboo's atmosphere. An elite group lands in the north of the planet, where Theed and the largest cities are found, while other groups target cities in the south and east. Each landing ship carries 11 MTTs (Multi-Troop Transports), 114 AATs (Armored Assault Tanks), and legions of droid troops. First to be deployed are droids on armed STAPs, who act as scouts for the main army, seeking out any signs of resistance—including two Jedi who have evaded capture.

ENTER THE NEIMOIDIANS

Only once Theed is under battle droid control do the invasion's perpetrators show their faces. Nute Gunray and his attaché, Rune Haako, affect the air of conquerors as they make the short walk from their shuttle to Theed Palace to personally oversee the arrest of Queen Amidala and her government. Being naturally cautious and lazy, the Neimoidians rarely leave their ships, relying on droids to meet customers. But in this instance, they are keen to visit the palace for themselves, having been advised that its staterooms are full of priceless treasures.

THE FALL OF THEED

With its citizens rounded up into detention camps and its streets sealed, Theed becomes a ghost town, echoing only with the sounds of tanks rumbling and troops marching. The city's long era of peace and serenity has ended in a matter of hours. Queen Amidala and her staff are escorted from the palace by droid captors taking them to a camp. But even in her darkest hour, the Queen refuses to abandon hope. She knows she will need some extraordinary help from somewhere if her beloved home is to be saved.

ADVANCE OF EVIL

The invasion force that advances upon Theed in the sharp light of a Naboo early morning comprised 33 large transports, each carrying 112 battle droids and 342 battle tanks, as well as droid starfighters and infantry. Each vehicle and battle droid is pre-programmed with a ground map of the city, with specific instructions for key objectives.

DEFENSE OF NABOO

WHEN THE TRADE FEDERATION INVADES NABOO, it expects little resistance from the planet's peace-loving inhabitants. But the invaders underestimate the courage and determination of its principal species, the Naboo and the Gungans, who overcome their traditional antipathy to form an unlikely alliance in the face of the emergency. The chief advantage the natives have is knowledge of the terrain. The Gungans amass a huge army in the swamps to lure the droid forces away from Theed, while the Naboo utilize hidden passages to infiltrate the palace and hangar, enabling them to mount attacks on multiple fronts.

While the inhabitants of Naboo struggle to rescue their planet from Trade Federation control, Qui-Gon Jinn and Obi-Wan Kenobi battle for their lives against a Sith warrior who appears to have an agenda all his own.

SYMBOLIC MEETING PLACE
Naboo and Gungan leaders plan their battle strategy on the dividing line between Naboo and Gungan lands. Long considered a no-man's-land, a refuge for outcasts like Jar Jar Binks, the swamp edges will play host to regular Freedom of Naboo celebrations in years to come.

SEARCH FOR THE GUNGANS
Traversing through dense swampland along nearly impenetrable paths known only to Gungans, Jar Jar Binks guides the Naboo and Jedi to the Gungan sacred place. When they near the hidden entrance, Jar Jar is unsure of the protocol for allowing outsiders into such a restricted zone and uses a Gungan call to alert scouts to his presence. The path threads its way beneath a thick canopy of ancient trees until the party emerges in a dry clearing filled with Gungan refugees. The Gungans gather at their sacred place in times of anxiety and apparent danger. These evacuations prove to be valuable practice when the time comes for a genuine emergency.

SECRET OPERATIONS
On Captain Panaka's instructions, Theed's underground resistance movement infiltrates the hangar in advance of its liberation. Secretly, officers and guards have checked that their fighters have not been disabled by battle droids. They have also restored access to the hangar computer system in order to program battle flight-path coordinates.

GROUND WAR

Although the Naboo people are rounded up into camps en masse, the Gungans prove more difficult to reach. By the time the invading battle droids reach Otoh Gunga and the other underwater cities, they find them nearly empty and most of the Gungan populace evacuated. Convening in the swamps, the Gungans raise an army large enough to challenge Trade Federation troops on the Great Grass Plains, buying Panaka's soldiers some much-needed time.

SPACE BATTLE

Naboo's pilot squadron, Bravo Flight, led by Ric Olié, is assigned the daunting task of knocking out the transmitter aboard the Droid Control Ship orbiting Naboo. Its combined fire power barely gets through the Control Ship's deflector shields. However, a reckless spin causes a split-second breach and Anakin's craft shoots into the righthand hangar arm toward the heart of the enemy.

1 In the first stages of the battle, the energy shield is vital to the protection of the Gungan army. A string of well-placed shield generators, carried by swamp lizards called fambaas, generate protection for troops stretching as wide as a kilometer (0.6 mile).

Energy shield

Kaadu-mounted cavalry protect vital fambaas

2 Encased within the energy shield, Gungan soldiers can do nothing but wait and hope that the barrier holds out against the relentless assault. When the laser battering halts, the Gungans are relieved, believing the battle is won.

Foot soldiers are organized into command units, each led by a general

Fambaa carrying energy shield

First rank formed by a row of AATs (battle tanks), supported by MTTs (large transports)

Laser-cannon beams repulsed by energy shield

12:00

Army on defensive ridge

Command Officer OOM-9 in AAT

Battle tanks withdraw as MTTs take their place — 12:10

12:15

Racks of folded-up battle droids slide out from the opened doors of MTTs

Battle droids reconfigure into standing position and form units of 56

On command from OOM-9, droid units advance in formation

MTTs close in to trap Gungan army

SHIELD GENERATOR

In the distant past, Gungan shield generator technology was used in defense against giant swamp creatures and sea monsters. It is maintained today as a symbol of Gungan military pride. The energy field is produced when an emitter, carried by one fambaa, fires a stream of plasma into a projector, carried by another fambaa.

Gungan operator controls size of dome

Plasma stream from emitter enters first drum, then shoots back and forth between the two drums to build up pressure before being forced upward through release chamber

Pressure coils

Release chamber

Excess heat vents

Battle droids march through perimeter of energy shield and begin firing

Gungans attack a battle tank

Shield generator apparatus destroyed by enemy laser fire

Falumpasets pull battle wagons loaded with energy balls for use in catapults

Jar Jar unwittingly releases a wagon load of energy balls

Retreating Gungan on kaadu

GRASS PLAINS BATTLE

THE CONFRONTATION BETWEEN Gungan troops and Trade Federation droids takes place 40 kilometers (25 miles) from Theed. On the morning of the battle, Gungan troops assemble under cover of the swamps. Soon after, the Neimoidians are alerted to the military buildup by rumors spread deliberately by Captain Panaka. The Gungan strategy is to wait until the droid army emerges from Theed to meet them on their own ground—in a spot near enough to the swamps to allow a hasty retreat if necessary. The plan works: by midday, two immense armies face each other across a shallow valley between ridges of low hills...

3 Deprived of an easy victory over the Gungans, Trade Federation battle tanks fall back. Agonizing moments of silence follow as MTTs (large transports) advance and begin unloading rack after rack of deadly battle droids.

GUNGAN BATTLE STRATEGY

Realizing that the Trade Federation's military might is far superior to their own, the Gungans plan to protect their army within a huge energy shield. The liquid energy surface repels laser bolts and large, slow-moving objects like tanks. Denied the option to wipe out the Gungans with their heavy artillery, the enemy is forced to send in individual battle droids. This gives the Gungans a fighting chance of engaging the droids long enough for the Naboo to capture the Viceroy.

12:20

12:25 — Droidekas in wheel configuration roll into battle alongside MTTs

12:30 — Battle tanks advance in pairs

12:35 — Troop carrier transports reserve droids to battle

12:40

4 Gungan energy balls, filled with high-voltage plasma, burst open on impact, short-circuiting battle droids and droidekas. These weapons are fired from catapults or flung from cestas and atlatls—and are sometimes released accidentally.

Cluster of droid command officers

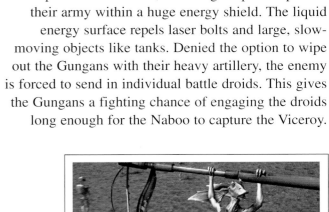

5 Amid the chaos of battle, no one is more confused than Jar Jar Binks. Attempting to flee, he is thrown off his kaadu onto the laser cannon barrel of an AAT. Captain Tarpals draws up alongside to save him, wasting valuable time in the process.

Battle droid rear guard, ready to take the places of fallen droids

Droideka in combat stance, twin blasters firing

12:50

MTTs remain a fearsome presence throughout battle

Piles of battle droids destroyed by Gungan catapults

In thick of battle, Gungan command units are broken up

Collapse of shield generators leaves Gungan army vulnerable to laser fire from MTTs

Repair droids ready to salvage reusable droid parts

Battle droids hit by energy balls

Battle droids round up prisoners

Individual Gungans carry out desperate counter-attacks

6 Just when it seems that the battle is lost, every battle droid suddenly falls inert as their control signals are severed. Initial Gungan disbelief soon gives way to jubilation and gentle retaliation, as Gungans discover the joys of "droid tipping"!

GENERATOR BATTLE

With its sleek, mechanistic interior lines, Theed's immense power generator stands in stark contrast to the city's elegant, handcrafted aesthetic. Indeed, this ingenious feat of engineering is now a popular attraction in Theed. The gigantic machinery works day and night to mine and stabilize naturally occurring plasma from deep within the planet. The Naboo people rely on this plasmic energy, using it for trade and to power their own cities, spacecraft, and even the glowing bulbs on Queen Amidala's Throne-Room gown. During the Battle of Naboo, the power generator becomes the scene of a climactic battle between Darth Maul and the Jedi Qui-Gon Jinn and Obi-Wan Kenobi.

As Obi-Wan hangs on to a security beacon within the power generator's core tunnel, Darth Maul lashes out with his lightsaber.

BREAK WITH THE PAST

For centuries, Theed's energy supply was provided by small outlying mines. However, evidence of a vast plasma source below the city's cliff face led to the construction of the new generator. Its efficient machinery mines much more than the city itself needs.

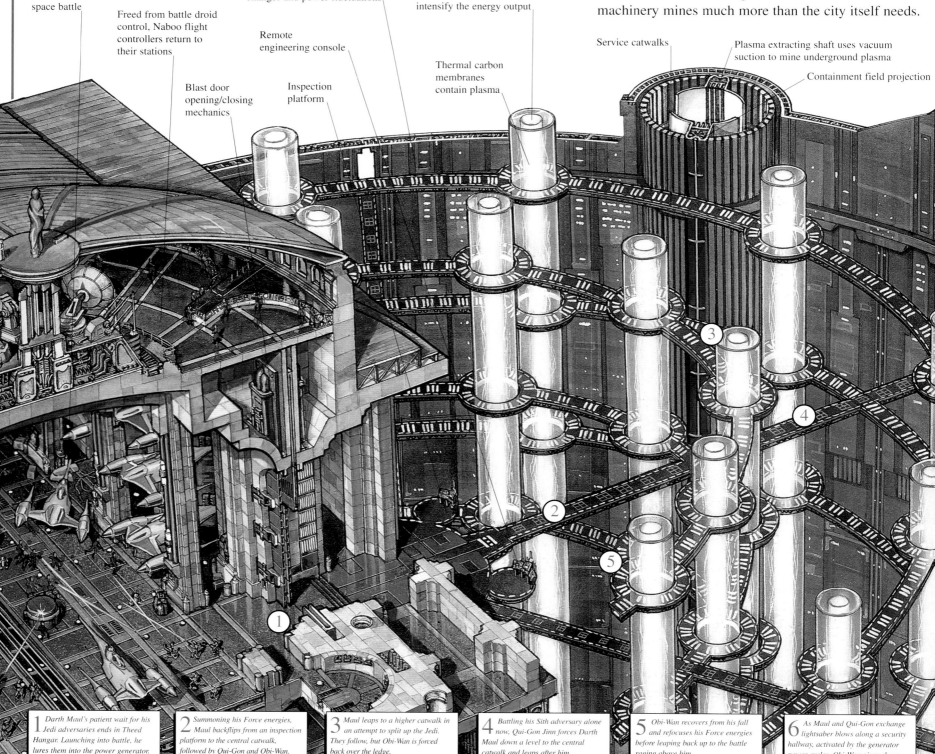

Theed Hangar is liberated and fighter pilots take off for space battle

Freed from battle droid control, Naboo flight controllers return to their stations

Panels constantly monitor and compensate for pressure changes and power fluctuations

Remote engineering console

Blast door opening/closing mechanics

Inspection platform

Plasma from extracting shaft is forced through each of the acceleration shafts in turn to intensify the energy output

Thermal carbon membranes contain plasma

Service catwalks

Plasma extracting shaft uses vacuum suction to mine underground plasma

Containment field projection

1 *Darth Maul's patient wait for his Jedi adversaries ends in Theed Hangar. Launching into battle, he lures them into the power generator.*

2 *Summoning his Force energies, Maul backflips from an inspection platform to the central catwalk, followed by Qui-Gon and Obi-Wan.*

3 *Maul leaps to a higher catwalk in an attempt to split up the Jedi. They follow, but Obi-Wan is forced back over the ledge.*

4 *Battling his Sith adversary alone now, Qui-Gon Jinn forces Darth Maul down a level to the central catwalk and leaps after him.*

5 *Obi-Wan recovers from his fall and refocuses his Force energies before leaping back up to the battle raging above him.*

6 *As Maul and Qui-Gon exchange lightsaber blows along a security hallway, activated by the generator power cycles, Obi-Wan gives chase.*

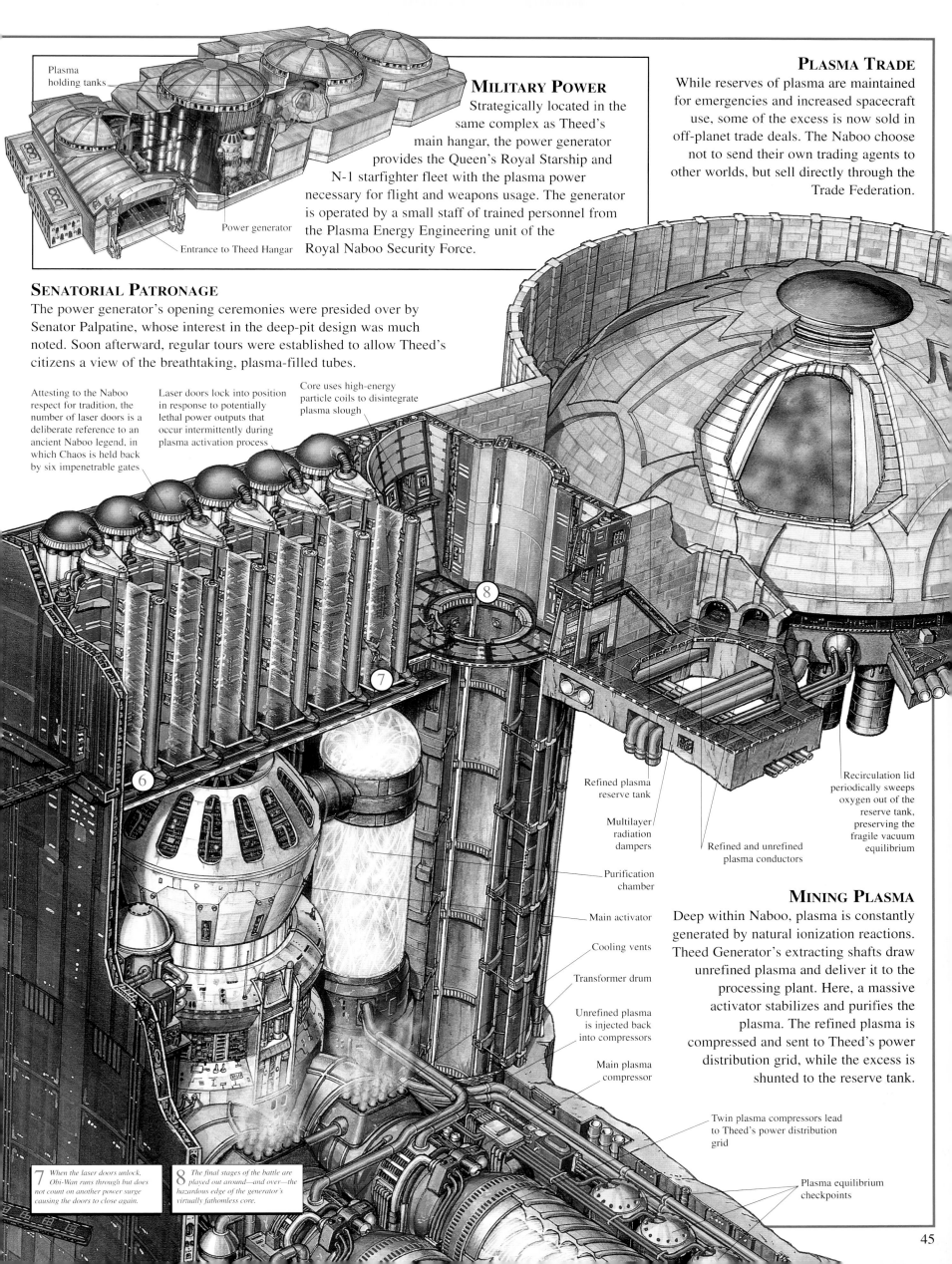

MILITARY POWER

Strategically located in the same complex as Theed's main hangar, the power generator provides the Queen's Royal Starship and N-1 starfighter fleet with the plasma power necessary for flight and weapons usage. The generator is operated by a small staff of trained personnel from the Plasma Energy Engineering unit of the Royal Naboo Security Force.

Plasma holding tanks

Power generator

Entrance to Theed Hangar

PLASMA TRADE

While reserves of plasma are maintained for emergencies and increased spacecraft use, some of the excess is now sold in off-planet trade deals. The Naboo choose not to send their own trading agents to other worlds, but sell directly through the Trade Federation.

SENATORIAL PATRONAGE

The power generator's opening ceremonies were presided over by Senator Palpatine, whose interest in the deep-pit design was much noted. Soon afterward, regular tours were established to allow Theed's citizens a view of the breathtaking, plasma-filled tubes.

Attesting to the Naboo respect for tradition, the number of laser doors is a deliberate reference to an ancient Naboo legend, in which Chaos is held back by six impenetrable gates

Laser doors lock into position in response to potentially lethal power outputs that occur intermittently during plasma activation process

Core uses high-energy particle coils to disintegrate plasma slough

Refined plasma reserve tank

Multilayer radiation dampers

Purification chamber

Main activator

Cooling vents

Transformer drum

Unrefined plasma is injected back into compressors

Main plasma compressor

Recirculation lid periodically sweeps oxygen out of the reserve tank, preserving the fragile vacuum equilibrium

Refined and unrefined plasma conductors

MINING PLASMA

Deep within Naboo, plasma is constantly generated by natural ionization reactions. Theed Generator's extracting shafts draw unrefined plasma and deliver it to the processing plant. Here, a massive activator stabilizes and purifies the plasma. The refined plasma is compressed and sent to Theed's power distribution grid, while the excess is shunted to the reserve tank.

Twin plasma compressors lead to Theed's power distribution grid

Plasma equilibrium checkpoints

7 When the laser doors unlock, Obi-Wan runs through but does not count on another power surge causing the doors to close again.

8 The final stages of the battle are played out around—and over—the hazardous edge of the generator's virtually fathomless core.

45

THE CITY OF THEED

WITH SQUADRONS OF BATTLE DROIDS patrolling the streets, battle tanks guarding access routes, and Trade Federation rulers holding the palace, Theed is a city under occupation. Yet, as a result of the quick capitulation of its populace, its buildings and monuments have remained relatively unscathed—most structural damage was caused by battle tanks steering through narrow streets. With all entrances and exits blocked, the small band of Naboo defenders has no choice but to use a hazardous network of underground passages to infiltrate their own city.

1 The defenders of Naboo use droid holoprojections to locate the secret routes into the city and the palace. These highly classified maps are stored in the Royal Starship's computers. The defenders emerge from the underground tunnels near the hangar.

2 Under Captain Panaka's command, Naboo soldiers in a Gian speeder blast at a Trade Federation tank regiment that is guarding the entrance to Theed Hangar. This courageous action diverts the droids away from the entrance.

Secret access to subterranean tunnels

One of the tributaries of the Solleu River

Boathouse

Royal Naboo Security Forces headquarters

Virdugo Plunge is the largest waterfall in Theed

Hangar entrance

3 Taking advantage of the diversion caused by Panaka, the Jedi, Anakin, Amidala, and R2-D2 emerge from the corner of the hangar where they have been hiding and slip into the entrance. Panaka and his soldiers expertly dispatch the droids and join them.

Theed Generator

Cliff edge is stabilized by hidden tension field generators

Ellié Arcadium

Captain's Panaka's private residence

The Hall of Perri-Teeka, a monument to a legendary statesman

Officers' clubhouse

Pergola's Bridge has become the main crossing point over the Solleu, taking some of the strain off the more fragile Bassa Bridge, further downstream

UNDERGROUND TUNNELS

Like their Gungan counterparts, the Naboo have long made use of the porous qualities of their planet. The naturally forming subterranean tunnels that run underneath Theed were once made safe, extended, and carefully mapped, but have since fallen into disrepair. As head of security, Captain Panaka recently inspected these secret routes in and out of the city, but had no idea how useful they would become when their city was occupied.

4 With most droid squads needed at the Gungan battle, the hangar interior is not left well guarded. Yet warning signals from the droids that are hit alert the Command Officer of the breech and droidekas are swiftly dispatched.

5 Pockets of battle droids guard key buildings in Theed. Nevertheless, when the Naboo defenders cross the city to reach the palace, they find they can take advantage of the city's maze of hidden passageways and connecting skywalks.

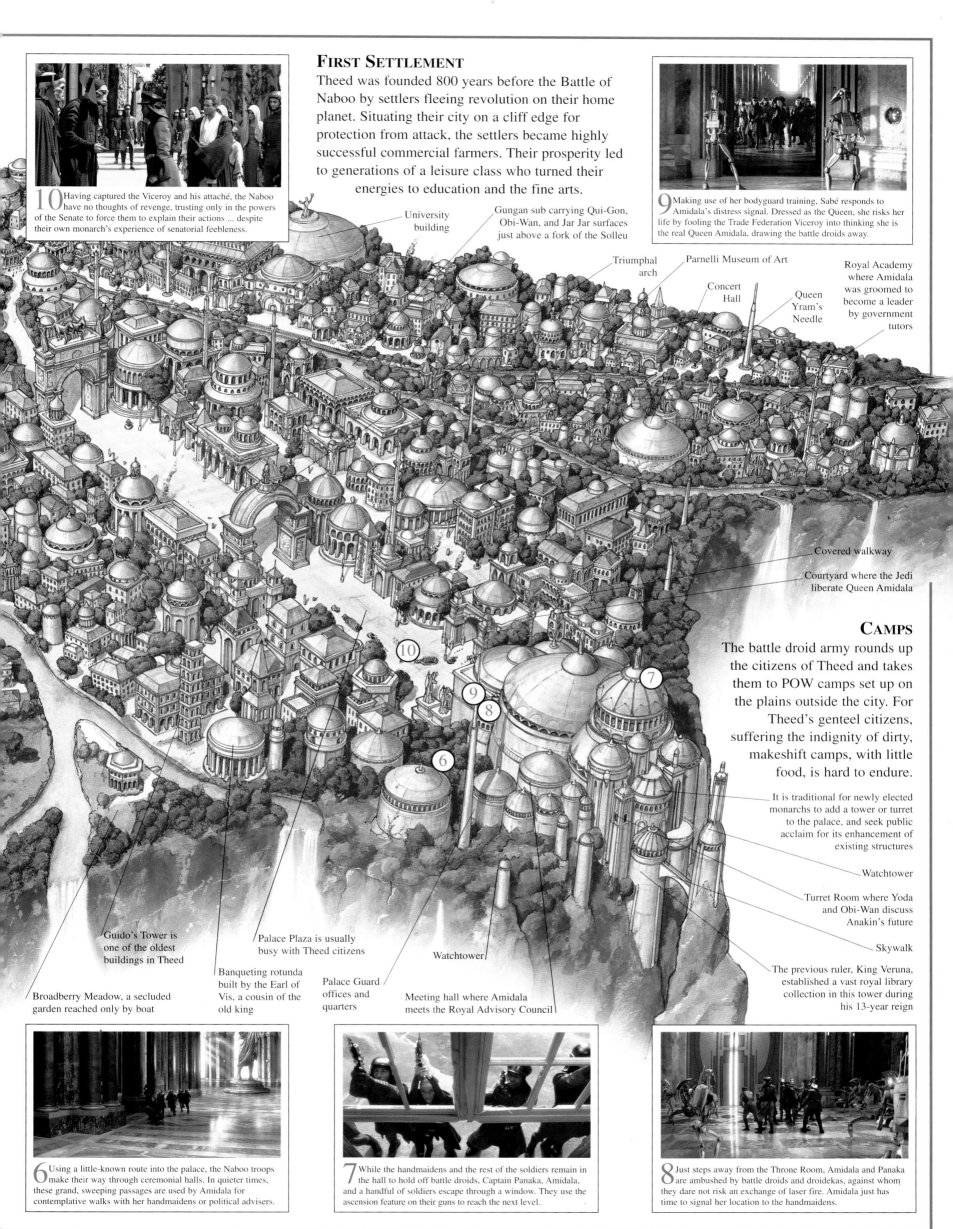

FIRST SETTLEMENT

Theed was founded 800 years before the Battle of Naboo by settlers fleeing revolution on their home planet. Situating their city on a cliff edge for protection from attack, the settlers became highly successful commercial farmers. Their prosperity led to generations of a leisure class who turned their energies to education and the fine arts.

10 Having captured the Viceroy and his attaché, the Naboo have no thoughts of revenge, trusting only in the powers of the Senate to force them to explain their actions ... despite their own monarch's experience of senatorial feebleness.

9 Making use of her bodyguard training, Sabé responds to Amidala's distress signal. Dressed as the Queen, she risks her life by fooling the Trade Federation Viceroy into thinking she is the real Queen Amidala, drawing the battle droids away.

University building

Gungan sub carrying Qui-Gon, Obi-Wan, and Jar Jar surfaces just above a fork of the Solleu

Triumphal arch

Parnelli Museum of Art

Concert Hall

Queen Yram's Needle

Royal Academy where Amidala was groomed to become a leader by government tutors

Covered walkway

Courtyard where the Jedi liberate Queen Amidala

CAMPS

The battle droid army rounds up the citizens of Theed and takes them to POW camps set up on the plains outside the city. For Theed's genteel citizens, suffering the indignity of dirty, makeshift camps, with little food, is hard to endure.

It is traditional for newly elected monarchs to add a tower or turret to the palace, and seek public acclaim for its enhancement of existing structures

Watchtower

Turret Room where Yoda and Obi-Wan discuss Anakin's future

Skywalk

The previous ruler, King Veruna, established a vast royal library collection in this tower during his 13-year reign

Guido's Tower is one of the oldest buildings in Theed

Palace Plaza is usually busy with Theed citizens

Watchtower

Broadberry Meadow, a secluded garden reached only by boat

Banqueting rotunda built by the Earl of Vis, a cousin of the old king

Palace Guard offices and quarters

Meeting hall where Amidala meets the Royal Advisory Council

6 Using a little-known route into the palace, the Naboo troops make their way through ceremonial halls. In quieter times, these grand, sweeping passages are used by Amidala for contemplative walks with her handmaidens or political advisers.

7 While the handmaidens and the rest of the soldiers remain in the hall to hold off battle droids, Captain Panaka, Amidala, and a handful of soldiers escape through a window. They use the ascension feature on their guns to reach the next level.

8 Just steps away from the Throne Room, Amidala and Panaka are ambushed by battle droids and droidekas, against whom they dare not risk an exchange of laser fire. Amidala just has time to signal her location to the handmaidens.

47

A DK PUBLISHING BOOK
www.dk.com

DORLING KINDERSLEY

SENIOR ART EDITOR John Kelly

DESIGNERS Guy Harvey & Keith Newell

MANAGING ART EDITOR Cathy Tincknell

DTP DESIGNER Jill Bunyan

SENIOR EDITOR Simon Beecroft

ASSOCIATE EDITOR David John

PUBLISHING MANAGER Karen Dolan

PRODUCTION Jo Rooke and Chris Avgherinos

LUCASFILM LTD.

ART EDITOR Iain Morris

MANAGER OF IMAGE ARCHIVES Tina Mills

EDITOR Sarah Hines Stephens

ASSOCIATE EDITOR Ben Harper

First American Edition, 2000

2 4 6 8 10 9 7 5 3 1

Published in the United States by DK Publishing, Inc.

95 Madison Avenue, New York, New York 10016

Library of Congress Cataloging-in-Publication Data

Lund, Kristin.

Star Wars. episode 1 : incredible locations / written by Kristin Lund : illustrated by Hans Jenssen & Richard Chasemore. - - 1st American ed.

p.   cm.

Summary: Text and cross-section illustrations describe the places seen in the "Star Wars, Episode I" movie, including the Jedi Council and Anakin's hovel.

ISBN 0-7894-6692-9 (hc.)

1. Star Wars, episode I, the phantom menace (Motion picture)--Miscellanea Juvenile literature. [1. Star Wars, episode I, the phantom menace (Motion picture)] I. Jenssen, Hans. 1963- ill. II. Chasemore, Richard, ill. III. Title.

PN1997.S6595L86   2000

791.43'72--dc21

99-39927

CIP

Reproduced by Colourscan, Singapore
Printed and bound by L. Rex, China

HANS JENSSEN painted Theed Hangar, Anakin's Hovel, Jedi Temple, Theed Overview, and Generator Battle.
RICHARD CHASEMORE painted Otoh Gunga, Watto's Junkshop, Podrace Circuit, Mos Espa Arena and Pit Hangar, Galactic Senate, and the shield generator.
ADDITIONAL ARTWORK BY: Roger Hutchins, Bill Le Fever

Acknowledgements

The author would like to thank all the people who made this book possible: Lucy Autrey Wilson and Fiona Macmillan, for giving me a shot at joining the *Star Wars* scribe club; Sarah Hines Stephens, for supplying me with all the resources a writer could need; Iain Morris, whose cheery voice was just the ticket on many an occasion; Simon Beecroft, for striking a balance between listening to his author and having an opinion of his own; John Kelly, whose vision of each spread before they had been drawn or written was inspirational; Richard Chasemore, whose artistic talent, energy, and vision are awe-inspiring; Hans Jenssen, who became a father while giving birth to his amazing illustrations; Jo Donaldson and Jenny Craik of the Lucasfilm Research Library for their help and enduring friendship; Ben Harper, whose *Star Wars* continuity expertise was invaluable; Tina Mills and Image Coordinators Scott Carter and Matthew Azeveda for the speed and efficiency with which they procured images for us; Anne Barson at LucasArts Entertainment, for getting me information on a number of occasions; Kathleen Phelps, a good friend and architect, who lent her design expertise; Lia Lund, Charm and Phil Meyer, and Scott Kivel, for looking after my daughters; lastly, my husband Michael, who was there when I needed him, gave me the extra time when I had to have it, and is the light of my life.

Hans Jenssen would like to thank Janine Morris; Richard Chasemore would like to thank Hilary Craig for her help and support throughout the project.

Dorling Kindersley would also like to thank: Doug Chiang and Robert Barnes in the Lucasfilm Art Department for their help and generous encouragement; Allan Kausch, Sue Rostoni, Steve Sansweet, Pablo Hidalgo, and Stacy Mollema at Lucasfilm for their attention to detail; Dr. David West Reynolds for his pioneering influence.

www.starwars.com
www.starwarskids.com